Divided Souls

Divided Souls

Tara L. Thompson

ISBN-13: 978-0692532713
ISBN-10: 0692532714

This book is dedicated to the wonderful people of my hometown, Chester, SC and also the great folks of Rock Hill, SC. Thank you for all your love and support! Small towns produce AMAZING things!!

Acknowledgements

Without God I am nothing, so I must give him all honor and praise. I thank him for my gifts, talents, and the platform he has provided me. God has blessed me beyond measure and I am indeed grateful. Thanks to my parents, Pastor W.W. Thompson and Diann Thompson, and my sisters, Tonya and Tiona, for always being there and supporting me. Thanks to my daughter, Sydney, for keeping a smile on mommy's face. Whenever I have a bad day I can always count on you to make it into a good day. Special thanks from my heart to my King. Thank you for your love, support, and pushing me to be better than the best. God and purpose baby!

Last year when I published Before I Say I Do, I never imagined the response I would receive. I want to thank all the book clubs that read my debut novel and the feedback that was given. Thanks to all my family, friends, fans, and supporters for purchasing my first novel and giving my work a chance.

Special thanks to the radio station V101.9 and Ms. Jennifer Hall for the featured article as a new author. Another special thanks to Traci Young Fant for having me on her show Real Talk with Traci Fant. Thank you to Travis Commodore, Ericka Howze, Terrance Wright, Richard Jamison, Michael Bailey and Minority Eye, Demarcus Crank and Let's Get It Management, James Thompson, Nick

Wright, Demorrious Robinson and Higher Definition Radio for opening your doors to me for book signings and interviews.

A huge heartfelt thank you to my great editors, Dr. Maxine Thompson and Felicia S. W. Thomas. Thank you both for the hard work on this project. Another special thank you to Mrs. Barbara Joe Williams for the blog appearance, referring me to an awesome editor, proofreading my work, and the support and guidance. My connection with you has truly been a blessing.

Special thanks to my cousin, Sherry Walker and my sister, Tonya Thompson for traveling to the many book festivals and assisting me with everything. Both of you have been there from the beginning and I love yall. A very special thank you to my creative advisor, Ms. Meredith Talford. Your creativity is unparalleled to anyone I have ever worked with and I appreciate your hard work on making my visions a reality. Another heartfelt thanks to Mr. Reeno Bowser, my model for the cover, and Memories By Morris for capturing my vision. Also, thank you to my test readers, LaShara McCrorey, Curtis Little, and both my sisters.

Thank you to everyone that has read my work, supported me, and told others about my books. I love all of you and will continue to give you the best of me.

Tara L. Thompson

Prologue

"**N**O, NO, NO!" Pastor Simms shouted. "I will not condone that kind of talk in MY church! Everyone calm down right now!" The veins bulged in his neck as he frantically waved his lanky arms up and down. The New Zion Baptist Church Friday night meeting was wrapping up, but there was one issue that the members were openly at odds over and the crass words that were being thrown around the holy building were enough to enrage the pastor. Pastor Simms stood in front of the burgundy and metallic gold altar, desperately trying to get the congregation's attention as they continued to talk among themselves.

"Pastor, I know we're supposed to open our doors to everyone, but wrong *is* wrong!" Sister Lucille rolled her thick neck and beady eyes at the same time. Her tight, greasy, jet black curls shook as she stood to say her piece. She looked around the room, waiting for agreement from her church family, and then plopped down her 250-pound frame on the wooden pew.

"Mmm, hmm," Sister Margaret and Sister Patricia said in unison.

"It just don't go with what we believe, Pastor." Deacon Jeter stood with his cane and tapped it on the brick-colored carpet. "Are we really gonna let some lil' sissy back in this place? Young men walkin' round with them tight ole jeans on and lil' flower shirts wantin' to be gals just ain't right!" Deacon Jeter continued, showing his obvious disdain. He sat down as Sister Margaret gingerly patted him on the back to quiet him.

Pastor Simms closed his eyes, rubbed his temples, and in a calmer voice, asked the church members to settle down. "We are not God; therefore, He is the only one that can judge this young man. Who are we to turn him away?"

Pastor Simms was not completely for allowing Freddie to return to the church, but he couldn't tell him no and turn his back on him. Whether he was gay or not, God still loved him. Freddie had spent many years at New Zion Baptist Church leading the youth ministries and singing in the choir. Many suspected his homosexuality; however, no one judged him until he officially came out and brought his lover to church with him. Once Freddie confirmed that he was indeed in a relationship with a man, some church members openly ridiculed and chastised him so much that they eventually drove him away. Pastor Simms did everything in his power to stop the condemnation, but it continued and Freddie left New Zion. That was almost five years ago and Pastor Simms still didn't understand, even after his meeting with Freddie a few days ago, why Freddie was so determined to come back.

"We don't turn anyone away from God," Pastor Simms continued. "Deacon Jeter, what if this was your son? Sister Lucille, what if this was your grandson? Are you saying that you would tell them God does not love them and they can't come to church and worship Him?"

Silence descended upon the sanctuary and everyone's full attention was now on the pastor. Pastor Simms removed his black-wired, reading glasses and stared intently at each member.

"Who will cast that first stone? What we have to do is pray that God will take that spirit away from this young brother. We all have sinned. We can't become too holy to stop feeding others the word. That is not what New Zion Baptist Church is about."

There were a few rumbles and moans, but no one dared to debate with Pastor Simms. Relieved that everyone had finally quieted down, he took this moment to conclude the extended session.

After prayer and dismissal, Pastor Simms retreated to his study to get his belongings together before traveling home. Tonight had been one of the toughest church meetings he had endured in a while and, to say the least, he was drained.

He sat down in his black leather swivel chair, loosened his cobalt blue silk tie, and exhaled. He thought about how Freddie had come to him asking to join the church again. Pastor Simms stroked his gray and black beard and recalled the speech he had given to his congregation. It very well could have been anyone's son, even his own. He picked up the family portrait off the L-shaped, cherry wood desk and traced his middle finger over the sterling silver picture frame. He smiled at his three lovely kids—Monica, Rachel, and Daryl— and Deborah, his beautiful wife of forty-three years. He was swollen with pride at what responsible adults his children had become.

Glancing toward the ceiling and thanking God that Daryl wasn't like Freddie, Pastor Simms replaced the picture and rose from his chair. Pastor Simms loved all his children equally, but was closest to his son. Daryl was the spitting image of his father and even carried himself with dignity and respect of a preacher. Even though Daryl didn't follow in his footsteps into the ministry, Pastor Simms still boasted about his career as a physical therapist with the Atlanta Falcons football team. He was elated that, after chasing all the fast women in the church, Daryl was settling down and getting married the next day. Not only was Saturday Daryl's wedding day, but also his twenty-seventh birthday—a cause for great celebration.

Pastor Simms thanked God again for a heterosexual son. He grabbed his briefcase and walked out of his study. When he turned around to lock the door, he heard faint footsteps coming toward him. Everyone should have been gone already, but maybe Deacon Jeter was still there locking up the church, Pastor Simms thought. He proceeded down the hall towards the back door where his pewter gray Cadillac CTS was parked.

The footsteps were behind him now and getting closer. Pastor Simms stopped abruptly and peered into the darkened hallway.

"Deacon?" he nervously called out. The footsteps stopped. He called out more forcefully, "Deacon Jeter?" Still nothing. Pastor Simms' pace quickened as he headed towards the door once again.

As he put his hand on the door knob, a scream cut through the darkness and caused him to let out a light yell and turn around once again.

"Who's there?" Pastor Simms asked boldly.

The footsteps were coming towards him faster now, but still he could not see down the dark hallway. He reached in his pocket and gripped the gold tarnished handle of the butterfly pocket knife that he always kept on him. New Zion Baptist Church was located near several dangerous neighborhoods that were home to a few gangs, so he always carried some sort of protection. Pastor Simms grew up in the grimiest part of Charlotte, and even though he was a minister now, there was still some hood in him. He agreed with the saying—you can take the person out the hood, but not the hood out of the person.

He took two steps forward and gasped as a man ran towards him, grabbed his shirt, and fell to the floor. Pastor Simms pulled out his pocket knife and braced himself to fight off any more attackers. After a few seconds, he took a closer look at the man on the floor. The man's body was racked with convulsions, and his groans and moans sliced through the eerie silence of the darkness. Pastor Simms looked around for any other assailants before trying to identify the man. Then, he reached into his shirt pocket for his cell phone.

"I'm calling the police!" Pastor Simms shouted, as he noticed the bloody handprints on his shirt that were made visible by his cell phone light.

Hands trembling, he glanced down again and dropped his phone. Suddenly, he realized who the man was that now lay lifeless on the floor.

"Freddie?" Pastor Simms whispered.

1

Corey

CHARLOTTE, NC

*F*our years had passed and this woman was getting on my LAST damn nerves. Really, what was she fussing about now? Before my wife even walked into the house, I heard her on the porch complaining. I punched the green arrow on the remote twice, turning the volume up on the television in order to drain out her never-ending grievances. The screen door slammed and Rachel tumbled in with two plastic groceries bags in her left hand and one in the right.

"Damn!" she screamed as the screen door caught her heel before she had a chance to fully step inside the house. Dropping the bags to the floor, she bent over to grab her foot and continued to mutter curse words.

"You sho' you been to church this mornin?" I asked sarcastically from across the living room. "The good Pastor wouldn't be so keen wit' his daughter usin' such foul language."

I know I should have checked to see if was she all right, but instead, I turned my focus toward the television. I was relaxing with my feet up in my favorite, coffee brown recliner that I had had since college. The pregame show was going off and I couldn't wait to see what my Carolina Panthers were going to achieve this football season.

"Maybe if you had gotten your lazy ass off the chair and helped me, I wouldn't be here bleeding." She continued to nurse her wound. "And speakin' of church, you could have gone with me today, Corey!"

I took a deep breath, sat up slowly, and pushed in the bottom part of my recliner. I reluctantly stood from my cozy chair and walked towards the front door where the bags of groceries lay. "You need help with this or nah?" I asked, pointing at the food on the floor.

Rachel huffed and picked up the plastic bags without looking at me. Her heels clicked loudly on the hard wood floor as she sprinted past me into the kitchen. I guess her anger towards me made her forget that she had just hurt herself on the door. I wasn't going to argue with her, so instead, I ventured outside. Slamming the screen door behind me, I stood on my porch and surveyed my yard. My olive green, quickly-turning-brown grass had grown an inch taller and was in desperate need of being cut. The unkempt yard may have been one of the many reasons my wife had come in the house with so much attitude.

The homeowner's association would surely leave a note in our mailbox this week if the grass wasn't taken care of. We moved into Glen Oaks subdivision two years ago and this uppity neighborhood caused our budget to be tighter than a prostitute's skirt on payday. Part of the reason I bought this overpriced house was to atone for my horrible sin and to release some of the guilt I felt every day. I thought I could make up for the wrongs I had done by giving my wife all the materials things she desired, even if it was a struggle. Now, I had nothing but regrets for purchasing this two story, brick home in South Charlotte.

I sat down on my front porch, slowly breathed in and closed my eyes. I tilted my head back, and after a few seconds, exhaled, wishing that I was blowing out a ring of smoke over my head instead of just air.

I had stopped smoking years ago, but today, I craved a cigarette, preferably a Newport in the soft pack. I rubbed my thumb and index finger together as if I had one of those white sticks with the brown tip in my hand now. Maybe one cigarette would calm the thoughts I had of taking my wedding ring off and throwing it clear across my yard. I contemplated buying a pack, but starting that habit again when it was so hard to quit deterred me from moving off my porch and driving to the store.

I dismissed the desire for a square and turned my attention to the red ant that was traveling by the right side of my shoe. It made a path across my white and orange Jordan and scurried along, seemingly in a hurry to get back to its queen. It was a damn shame I wasn't in a rush to go back inside to mine. Pots and pans clashed together as my supposed "queen" rummaged around in the kitchen still grumbling about what I was doing, or worse, what I wasn't. I swear, sometimes, I wanted to tell her to just chill out—

everything is not that serious. But to my wife it was; everything was Armageddon to her.

This Sunday afternoon, the porch was my refuge and the white faux wood chair that held my 190-pound frame was my throne. The sun beat down on my chest as my thoughts drifted to that special day four years earlier. I recalled the overwhelming feeling I had when Rachel walked down the church aisle toward me. Tears fell freely from my eyes, despite my efforts to hold them back. I couldn't hide my emotions because this angelic being who was dressed in the most enticing white satin gown was slowly approaching me, and she was mine. I loved her more than I had ever loved anyone in my life.

The years came and went so quickly. It seemed like just yesterday we were on our honeymoon in Cancun making love all day, laughing, and talking like two teenagers.

However, no matter how sweet the memories were, yesterday was gone and we were living in today. As far as I could see, today sucked.

"Corey!" She called my name for the second time.

I heard her the first time she called me too, but I hoped that if I didn't answer, she would give up trying to get my attention. However, I had no such luck since she continued to yell my name. Again, I didn't answer her; did not give her a "yes dear", "what do you need baby", or a "huh". I didn't move. I remained silent, rested my chin on my fist, and watched a trail of ants climb along my black iron railing as they set off to do something important in their small world. However, in my world, I didn't want to do anything and answering my wife was definitely not on my to-do list.

My red oak front door decorated with stain glass windows at the top was ajar leaving only the rickety, abused screen door between us. It was damaged as a result of constantly slamming it after numerous arguments. The screen door desperately needed to be reattached to its hinges. It was yet another thing I knew she would complain about soon. If I had a dollar every time she griped about something, I would be a wealthy man.

A few minutes had passed since she called my name and I still hadn't responded. I was certain she knew I had heard her, and even more sure she was aware that I was ignoring her. I wanted to scream out, "Why the hell do you keep calling my name?" However, I wasn't a complete idiot. That would only lead to another fight and more problems than I cared to have. Finally, the noise in the kitchen stopped. An uncomfortable silence seeped from the house. I glanced toward the screen door and saw her standing there watching me, still with a disgusted look on her once pleasant face.

"Guess you're deaf now, huh?"

"You called me?" I asked. I assumed she knew that I had heard her but there was no reason for me to admit that I was disregarding her.

"Don't play with me, Corey. You know damn well you heard me calling you."

This time, I didn't say anything. I just looked at my wife. She frowned and stared back at me. I was so used to seeing her scowl that it didn't even bother me anymore. It was normal.

"So what'cha want?" I tried to turn my mouth up into a smile, but only one side lifted and it probably looked like a half smirk instead.

"I *wanted* you to help me in the kitchen, Corey." Rachel rolled her eyes and placed her hands on her hips—the hips that I use to love so much; the hips that I spent countless nights gripping while she was on top of me moving back and forth. My wife's tantalizing hips were masked now by a faded pair of blue jogging pants and an oversized white t-shirt that she had changed into while I was sitting outside. Nothing about her outfit, or the way she addressed me, made me want to help her or even be around her. I would have preferred she kept on the short, grey skirt and white and grey, low-cut blouse that she had worn to church. Ironically, she would get dressed up for the Lord but would look her absolute worse for the husband whom she saw every day.

"Oh, soooo now you want my help? I coulda sworn I just asked you that before I came outside," I snapped.

"Whatever, Corey," Rachel hissed before she stomped back towards the kitchen. She continued whatever she had been doing before she interrupted my thoughts. Whatever important task she was engaged in, she was back at it, pounding on pans and throwing pots.

Thankful that she had left me alone, I exhaled and closed my eyes again. All I longed to do was watch Sunday football.

I envied the men who sat in front of their large, flat screen televisions mounted high on their living room walls, cheered on their favorite teams, and relaxed with a cold beer in their hands. That's exactly how my Sunday should have been. Instead, I was sulking on my front porch, wanting to be anywhere but here.

Even though I was beyond discontented at the moment, I can't say that I was miserable every day. There were times that I felt love for my wife, and when we were snuggled in bed, my heart got closer to hers and I was at peace. She would give me a slight smile and I took in the CoCo Chanel perfume she always wore. Maybe we needed to stay in bed all the time since, as soon as our feet hit the floor and we opened the door to reality, we glared at one another again. We fought over bills and housework. The never ending argument over my work schedule was enough to drive a wedge between two people who vowed to love each another forever. Today, all my frustrations were coming to a head, leaving me on my porch filled with dread before I walked back into my house.

The sun roasted me and drained the tiny bit of energy that I had before I wandered outside. An hour of the sun had my "wife beater" stuck to me as if it was an extension of my skin. My knee-length, khaki shorts felt even heavier now that they were wet from sweat. My arms were sticky and my legs appeared a shade darker than my usual golden brown color. I ran my hand over my low top fade and wiped the perspiration that had gathered on my forehead. However, I would rather endure many days of the September humidity than the heat that was currently spewing from my wife.

She had gone to church without me and came back with all this anger bottled up inside and ready to erupt as if everything wrong in the world was my fault. Most people left church full of joy and ready to minister to others; but, oh no, not my wife.

She was carrying on like she had been to a funeral rather than morning church service. Maybe it was because I didn't go to church with her. I didn't even go every Sunday. I worked on some Sundays, and on others, I was just too tired. I was the district manager for the Target Retail Stores and it was very demanding. During most weeks, Sunday was the only day I had off, so the majority of the time, I just slept late.

As I sat outside depressed, she was in the kitchen banging everything around attempting to cook dinner in the loudest manner possible. I was sure all that noise was to disturb me, but as long as I didn't have to hear her mouth, I was fine. The scent of fried chicken flowed from the open kitchen window. The aroma of my favorite food was wasted since the run-in with my wife made me lose my appetite. This definitely was not the life that I had envisioned for us.

My vibrating phone distracted me and I reached into my khakis to retrieve it. I squinted to see the message through the blinding sun. It was a picture text, and since I already knew who it was from, I decided not to open it. My wife was known to creep here and there. The last thing I needed was for her to see what she surely would not understand.

I sat my phone in my lap, rested my head on the back of the lawn chair, and closed my eyes once more. Four years lying and hiding something that could tear us apart was exhausting, but there was no other option. I made so many awful choices that I couldn't even start to mend them. I knew that it would be mere minutes before my cell phone would start ringing. Sure enough, only about five minutes after the text, it began to ring. I looked down and saw a number pop up on my screen. Even though the number wasn't saved in my phone, I didn't have to guess who was calling—the one person that could end my marriage and make me lose everything; the one person I hated with every fiber of my being. Unbeknownst to my wife, that person had her future and mine in the palm of their hands and they let me know this every chance they got.

2

Rachel

CHARLOTTE, NC

*G*od was punishing me. Yeah, that sounded about right; I was being punished. I slammed the three bags of groceries on the kitchen counter and kicked off my black and grey platform heels. The back of my foot was still sore, but at least the bleeding had stopped. I had just returned from morning service, and no matter how much I went to church, I still felt like I was being repaid for what I had done. That was the only reason I could think of that would explain why I was going through hell right now. I was getting what I deserved for sleeping with, and getting pregnant by, a married man.

The pregnancy ended painfully in miscarriage. The torture of enduring a miscarriage was, I believed, my retribution. Sadly, I was mistaken, since I was still going through so much turmoil. Knowing that the baby was not Corey's, I probably should have been relieved that the miscarriage occurred. There was no chance it could have been his. We were living in two different cities at the time and rarely saw each other. When we spent time with one another all we did was fight, not having much desire on either parts to make love. However, I wasn't granted that feeling of ease with the loss of my child. I only felt a heart-aching void that still had not been filled.

It happened four years ago, right before my wedding. I tried to be the same Rachel that I was before the affair—the Rachel that was completely in love with my soon-to-be husband, Corey, and wanted just him. I pretended well, and after the wedding, for two years, I believed that I had fallen in love with Corey all over again. We had our difficult periods with planning the wedding, but once we said those vows, it seemed like everything was on track again. Maybe it had and it just didn't last.

Recently, there were nights when Corey was snoring and I got out of bed and wandered in the living room. I would curl up on our cream suede sofa, close my eyes, and wait until I saw him; wait until that vision made its appearance. He was the essence of a real man wrapped in a smooth, dark, chocolate skin tone. His aura glowed like a light around him as he stepped into my sight. His newly-shaved, bald head gradually came into view. His piercing eyes could read into the depths of my soul. I feared I might whisper his name in my sleep, so I prayed that Corey would not hear me if I did. I hoped he would not hear me utter the name of the man who made love to me four years ago and planted his seed inside me. In my dream, I could see him, smell him, and feel him. He would walk over to me and gently touch my face, and I would speak his name. I opened my mouth and his name flowed out of it. Terrence.

A cold chill traveled down my spine and made it feel like forty degrees in my house instead of the actual seventy degrees. For a moment, I forgot about the pan that I just slammed on the stove. The anger I felt after walking into a dirty house and seeing my husband relaxing with his feet up acting as if he didn't have a care in the world dissipated. I even dismissed the pain from that damn screen door closing on my heel. How could one man make me feel like this even after all these years? One man who was not my husband. How was this even possible?

Prior to my wedding, I experienced more stress than I had ever had in my life. From the wedding plans to arguments with Corey about any and everything, and dealing with my mom and mother-in-law, made me depressed, lonely and desperate for love. Then entered Terrence Walker. I was working at my current job, Lawry & Snyder Law Firm, as the Business Office Manager, and Terrence was a lawyer at our sister law firm in Atlanta, Georgia. What started out as an innocent friendship ended as a full-fledged affair. I smiled as I thought about the many conversations Terrence and I had that made my heart soar.

My ringing cell phone suddenly interrupted the thoughts of my past lover. I carefully hopped over to the couch and rummaged through the mess in my purse to find my phone. The face of my older sister, Monica, flashed on the phone before it disappeared and the message "one missed call" appeared. I pressed call back to see what Monica wanted. I was surprised that she was calling me only an hour after we had left each other at church. This could only mean that something had happened in my sister's never-ending, melodramatic life. I carried the phone and my purse into the bedroom so I could change out of my church clothes into something more comfortable.

The phone rang twice and my sister's screeching voice interrupted the quietness of my house. I quickly turned the volume down to avoid the headache that I seemed to always get from talking to her on the phone.

"Sis, wait 'til I tell you what this slut did now!" Monica screamed, excited and out of breath at the same time.

I immediately knew she was referring to Sheka, her husband Tony's baby momma, once she said "this slut." Monica and Tony had been married a little over two years.

After dating my sister for almost a year, dogging her out, and learning an ex-girlfriend of his was pregnant with his child, he gave his life to God and asked Monica to marry him. No one in my family accepted Tony at first, but once he was saved, we all tolerated him more. However, tigers never change their stripes. Tony was proving that saying to be very true. The family learned that, right after making Monica his wife, he resumed his old habits of staying out all night and cheating. Not only was he up to no good, he had a baby momma from hell. She made sure that she did everything possible to guarantee there was absolutely no happiness in my sister and Tony's life.

"Sis, I may need some cash from you tomorrow. How much can you spare 'til my payday?" Monica asked.

"Monica, what happened?"

"Girl, now you already know Tony ain't got no license, right? Last night, this broad spray painted on the trunk of his

car 'POLICE PLEASE STOP ME! I HAVE NO LICENSE.'
The chick so dumb, she even spelled license with a "y"."

"Monica, you serious?" Tony's baby momma, Sheka, was
ghetto as all hell, but this was a low blow even for her.

"YES!" Monica shouted. "The fool left this morning
before I went to church and didn't even realize that Sheka
wrote on his car until the police stopped him. They told him
he was pulled over for running a stop sign, but you know
what she wrote had something to do with it. As soon as they
found out his license was suspended, they took him in. He
just called from jail."

"I thought he was getting his license back this month."

"He was supposed to, sis," Monica whined.

"I had to pay the light bill, so we pushed getting his
license back 'til next month. He probably won't be able to get
'em back no time soon after this."

"So what y'all gonna do?" I hoped that she wouldn't ask
me for money again, but that was just wishful thinking since
it was the purpose of her call.

"Rach, I need some money. I'm broke as hell and Tony
just started with this bail bonding business shit. He ain't
making no money yet. Dumb ass ain't even allowed to bail
his own self out of jail. I mean, really, sis! Why be a
bondsmen if you can't help your own damn self?"

I tried to hold my laughter in, but somehow a chuckle
slipped.

"It ain't funny, Rachel!" Monica screamed. "I am so sick
of dealing with this bullshit from him and especially dumb ass
Sheka!"

"Aight, calm down, Monica. I'll see what I can do. Things are tight around here too, but we might can help out a little."

"Thanks, girl. I will hit you back later once I know how much it will be. Love ya, sis."

"Love you, too," I told Monica.

Shaking my head, I placed my phone in my purse and walked out of the bedroom and into the kitchen to finish cooking. Corey was sitting outside now and I didn't want to talk to him, especially about money. The fact that he didn't help me with the groceries and could have cared less when I hurt myself was enough for me to give him the silent treatment for the remainder of the day. He handled all our bills, so he would know if there was any extra money in our account. I never had a reason to look at the finances, but in order to avoid asking him to help my sister, I decided to take a look later to see if there was anything we could do for her.

Monica's job as a bill collector at a small insurance company didn't pay much. Tony was always job hopping, causing the majority of the bills to be Monica's responsibility.

Corey and I didn't have the same money issues as Monica and Tony. I was approaching my seventh year as the Business Manager at the law firm. I made a modest salary; however, Corey made more as a district manager. Since he was the dominant breadwinner, I didn't interfere with our finances. Lately though, Corey fussed more and more about sticking to the budget he had prepared. The finances were another argument that Corey and I constantly had.

Corey sat on the porch sulking like an overgrown child. I hoped he would leave for a few hours like he did usually after we argued. I wanted to be alone with my thoughts and fantasies of Terrence. I hadn't spoken to Terrence in years, but the memories of our time together were as permanent and significant as childhood events. I still felt like a love-struck school girl when I thought about the things that happened before I said I do.

I snapped out of my daydream once I smelled the stench of burnt rice on the stove. I ran over to the stove, turned the eye off, and moved the pot to the sink. Thankfully, my lack of focus hadn't caused me to burn the chicken that was evenly frying in the pan next to the rice. As I tried to salvage the rice, I thought about how different my life could have been. I constantly wondered if I had made the right decision by marrying Corey. This was definitely not the happily-ever-after that I had dreamed of.

I opened the refrigerator, took three eggs out of the carton, and gently placed them on the counter. I steadied the eggs and faced the pot in the sink. One egg slowly rolled off the counter and splattered on the floor. The ruined contents mimicked my marriage—a shattered egg that could not be fixed or repaired. The only thing left to do was scrap it off the floor and put it in the trash. How in the world did my marriage get to this?

3

Von

ATLANTA, GA

"Mercy, please pick up your toys and take 'em in your room. My living room looks like your toy box threw up!" I stood in my kitchen watching my almost four-year-old daughter roll her eyes at me and slowly stand to pick up her stuffed alligator and monkey. Her long, brownish-red ponytails fell in her face as she stomped into her room to place her stuffed friends on her Hello Kitty purple and white twin bed.

"Mercy, hurry up!" I shouted as she dragged herself into the living room and slid her feet across the tan shag carpet. Her round, lemon-colored face scrunched up and she rolled her eyes a second time. She picked up her Doc McStuffins doll and trotted back to her room.

"Lil' girl, you have one mo' time to roll those eyes," I cautioned as she disappeared into her room. She was trying my patience today with all the faces and eye rolling, which made her look more and more like her father. Her complexion was two shades lighter than my dark mocha skin color, and even though she looked like her father, her personality was mine. She would be turning four in two months and she was a spitfire just like I was. As she returned to the living room to pick up the rest of her toys, my thoughts fell on her father.

I pressed "send" on my IPhone6, then flung it onto my beige tile kitchen counter. It landed face down with a thud.

If it wasn't for the OtterBox case, my screen could have easily been damaged. I realized that I wouldn't receive a response to my text, so there was no need to wait on an answer. A part of me, sometimes, was glad that he didn't respond. Then, there were those times, such as today, that I wished he would just say something. I wanted him to say anything other than the usual "money is in the account" that he sent by text on the first of each month. I lowered my head and glanced at my phone. I would have been more outraged if I had let my anger towards him cause me to break my new phone.

Either way, I was always frightened that the day would come when everything would be out in the open. I was scared to death of the thought that my secrets might be revealed. Ironically, I am not the type of person who has ever been afraid of much. As a matter of fact, my motto is the line from the old Bonecrusher song, "I ain't never scared." At least, that's how I used to be, but times had changed. I used to be bold and brazen. I did what I wanted and said what I felt. My infamous, devilish grin crossed my face as I reveled in the memories of the things I had been cocky enough to do. I slept with whomever I wanted, when I wanted, and used those losers until I dropped them with ease. The trifling, married men were the worst—they would sign over an entire check to me for a shot of ass. I chuckled when I thought about the last married man I dealt with a few years back.

His name was Thomas, but I called him "KM" for killa mouth. Thomas was the color of a yellow crayon with freckles sprinkled across his face. He was short and husky with arms that were disproportionate to the rest of his body. They looked as if they were too long for his build and should have been on a much leaner and taller person. Thomas wasn't gruesomely unattractive but he definitely wasn't someone that would normally get a second look from me.

He worked in the marketing department of Treasury Securities at Bank of America, which was located directly across the hall from the consumer loans business department that I worked in. Most days, either at lunch or at the end of the day, we would end up on the elevator together. I noticed his stares and the wedding ring on his finger. His charm and persistence made me overlook his stubbiness and marital status to take him up on an offer for dinner once he got up enough nerve to ask. The married men I normally dated had to be so smooth and dapper, no sane woman could turn them down. Thomas was obviously not what I was used to. However, his abilities allowed him to stay around for a while.

Thomas was the only man that I had ever been with that could wet me up and dry me out with only his tongue. He would use his tongue and satisfy me in ways I never thought possible. Thomas would go down on me and not come back up until his mouth was drenched with my juices and I had climaxed at least five times. After sex with anyone else, I always wanted more and would be just as wet and ready as I was before the encounter. However, I didn't need any other stimulation after Thomas and many times, I went to sleep right after showing him to the door. Most men would not be too keen with pleasing a woman and getting nothing in return, but not my KM. He was content with wrapping his hands around my ass and thrusting me in his mouth like I was Thanksgiving dinner. I kept him around just for that purpose. A few times, I rewarded him by letting him enjoy the warmth of my sweetness. His penis was nowhere as good as his mouth; therefore, letting him inside my walls was not a habit. He showered me with gifts and money, and even though I was not hurting for any cash, I didn't mind taking his.

My time with Thomas ended when his wife, who was just as simple as he was, started calling my phone. A giggle escaped me as I thought about how he begged and pleaded once I told him to lose my number. His mouth game was the only thing I would miss about him.

I ran my fingers through my pixie cut and glanced again at my phone still lying on the counter. The sight of it brought me back to reality and the present. I longed to be that same chick that had all the men falling at my feet. My looks were the same, but inside, I had changed tremendously. I was different due to the mistake I made that changed my entire life.

Of all the nonsense I had gotten myself into, I didn't know how I would get out of this predicament. The only thing I could do was live with this secret. Live with this lie. I had lied to myself so much that I actually started to believe it. It's pretty deep when you start believing your own lie. It took a long time for me to deal with it and I still had a hard time doing so. The exposure of my secrets and losing everyone I loved was constantly on my mind.

Given no other choice, I had to stay the course and continue this lie until I took my last breath. Maybe on my death bed, I would finally be able to rid myself of this weight and tell the truth. For all my deception, my fate would probably include me dying a quick death without even having the opportunity to rid myself of this guilt. Mercy was what I needed granted on me for all my sins and exactly why I named my daughter that.

Mercy was on her knees in the middle of the floor picking up her crayons. She tried to stuff them back into the box and got annoyed that they were not fitting neatly inside.

"Maaaa, I can't put dem in," Mercy whined, holding the crayons and box in the air. She lowered them and began cramming the crayons in two at a time.

Her pink and orange shirt, which was decorated with multi-colored butterflies, matched her pink tights and draped loosely over her slender frame. She was taller than most four-year-olds, but that wasn't a surprise. I stood at 5'10" and her dad was over six feet tall. I was about to tell Mercy to hurry up again until her dad's face flashed in my head. I tried not to think about him much, but today, it seemed like everything she did reminded me of him.

I walked out of the kitchen, leaving Mercy's jelly sandwich half made. I had forgotten to go grocery shopping to get more peanut butter, so this grape jelly sandwich would have to do for lunch and probably dinner as well. I slid through the living room of my two bedroom apartment, past my daughter on the floor, and over to the balcony door. I stepped over Mercy's plastic fruits and vegetables that belonged in her toy shopping cart and almost tripped over the Barbie doll that was lying beside them.

I closed my eyes and counted to ten before I spoke to Mercy again. My temper took control of me terribly and caused me to scream at her often. Then, the overflow of tears would come from my daughter and I would feel awful. I would hold her and tell her I would never do it again, but that was a lie.

"Baby, please get these toys up," I said in a calmer tone so Mercy would lose the attitude and clean up. I opened the blinds and watched the minute raindrops splatter against my patio door. The weather mirrored my current mood. The dismal sky opened, and in a matter of seconds, the downpour began to flood the view of my apartment's parking lot. I promised Mercy that we would go to the theater this Sunday afternoon to see the Disney movie, Home. I didn't want to disappoint her since I rarely took her places anyway, but the outside conditions, along with my attitude, caused me to want to just sit in the house all day. If Mercy had been with my mom, my sister Vivian, or at daycare, I would have languished the couch with my favorite liquor, peach Ciroc, and cried until I had no tears left or until it was time for her to return.

I peeked over my shoulder at my daughter on the floor. She had given up on the crayons and was now putting her plastic carrots and apples in her shopping cart. I thought back to when I first found out I was pregnant for the fourth time. Three abortions before Mercy had taken a toll on my body, and there was no telling what might happen if I had another one.

I reluctantly carried on with the pregnancy and the only thing left to do was leave my home in Charlotte, North Carolina.

My first thought was to run across country either to California or Washington State but I didn't want to be completely alone. After a few weeks of trying to figure out where I wanted to go, I settled on Atlanta and took a lateral position with Bank of America. My half-sister, Vivian, lived in Atlanta and we had become really close since our first meeting only a few years ago. She was an outside child of my father's and, in an attempt to right his wrongs, he introduced her to me and my brother, Kevin. Back then, I didn't want anything to do with Vivian, but over the years, I enjoyed getting to know her.

She had separated from her husband, Terrence, and my moving closer to her worked out great for both of us. She was a mother of three and needed help with the kids, and I also needed assistance with Mercy since I knew nothing about motherhood. My mom didn't want me to move initially, but once she saw how miserable I was in Charlotte, she told me to do whatever it took to make me happy. The only other person that took my move extremely hard was my best friend, Rachel. She gave me several reasons not to leave. I had sank further into depression and started drinking more than I even realized. Once Rachel saw that this move was needed so that I could get my life back, she quit objecting.

After I relocated, I told Rachel that I was pregnant. So many times, I wondered how Mercy was born healthy since I never stopped drinking during the pregnancy. I guess it really was in God's plan for me to have her. Having Mercy was the best and worst decision of my life. I love my daughter with all that is in me. I had never felt that kind of love before; never knew love so unconditional and so pure. Whenever she looked at me with her innocent eyes and open-mouthed smile, I knew she loved me.

Having her also meant living with the mistake I made— the one I was reminded of constantly and could never undo. Lives could be destroyed if this mistake was ever revealed. At times, I wanted to take my own life; the only reason I couldn't was walking back and forth picking her toys off the floor.

4

ATLANTA, GA

"Stop! Please . . . stop!" the boy wailed as the man yanked him by the neck with one hand and covered his mouth with the other. The man's breath reeked of a mixture of Seagram's Gin and Olde English beer. The smell of hot garbage that rose from his body was so intense, the boy nearly puked in the man's hand. His twelve-year-old hands tried to pry the man's massive, dirty and tart fingers from his mouth, but he was too strong. Tears poured from his eyes and stung the freshly bleeding cut on his cheek.

Lil Wayne's voice radiated from my cell phone, which was lying on the floor and woke me up from my lurid nightmare. Still trembling from the visions, I opened my eyes and tried to catch my breath. I quickly wiped the sweat beads from my forehead and shifted from my left side to the right in the recliner that was my bed for the night. I shook my head and erased the dream from my mind as my eyes focused on the body that was sprawled out in my bed. I kicked the corner of my California king-size bed to awaken the chocolate goddess who was snoring softly in my bed. She was lying on her side, away from me, exposing her smooth, firm ass. It was almost like she was calling out to me to come and take control of it like I had done hours earlier. I felt my joint stiffen as I thought about going another round with her.

Then again, she had already overstayed her welcome, which was the reason I slept in my recliner and not in the bed beside her. I didn't want to give her the impression there would be any cuddling or holding after our sex session. Most women would leave after we were done, but Chantal had gotten comfortable and fallen asleep in my bed. It was now time for her to go.

I had a breakfast date with my fianceé in a few hours and also a Monday night football game to prepare for. Three players were on the list for physical therapy and they would demand my full attention. Chantal wasn't worth being late to meet Briana or off my game tonight.

The previous night, I met Chantal, a 5'8, sexy, silky, dark-skinned lady, at one of the bars I frequented in downtown Atlanta. I was used to women approaching me, but when Chantal eased her gorgeous body on the barstool next to mine, I couldn't help but notice her. A few pleasantries were exchanged, and once I recognized the lust in her eyes, I invited her back to my place. That was four hours ago and I was restless and annoyed due to a lack of sleep.

I gazed at Chantal again in my bed and debated joining her and going another round. The knowledge that she would have a quick orgasm and then become a desert made my erection deflate. I frowned at the thought of fighting with the sandpaper between her thighs and hurting myself in the process. An idea popped into my mind and caused the blood to rush to my boxers. I left the recliner and approached the bed where her head lay on my black satin pillow. Ever so gently, I moved her long, thick, black hair from the front of her face. The shape of her slightly opened mouth made me even harder. I slid my boxers down, exposing my nine inches, and slowly eased the head towards her mouth. I didn't want to startle her into biting down on my meat, so I methodically traced her lips with the tip.

"Chantal," I whispered, tapping her top lip with my throbbing piece. "Chantal, wake up."

She slowly opened her hazel eyes and lit up once she realized what was brushing across her lips. Chantal lifted herself up on her elbows and immediately wrapped her fingers around my shaft, swallowing my entire penis. Saliva dripped from her mouth as she moved her head back and forth making loud slurping sounds. Every few seconds, I could hear her gather more spit in her mouth, and then drip it on me until I felt I was submerged under water.

My knees began to weaken as her movements became faster. Fearing that I would fall, I grabbed the top of her head to keep my balance, and guided her motions. I tilted my head back and moaned. I knew I was seconds away from releasing in her mouth. Sure enough, as if an electric current was running throughout my body from my feet and to my penis, I groaned and released everything I had into her mouth. As if she was acting in a pornographic movie, Chantal licked and slurped every drop of my substance like it contained supernatural powers she could not live without. Finally, my legs gave out and I tumbled on the bed beside her.

"Think I can get another one out you?" Chantal whispered, revealing her deep New York accent. She ran her fingers up and down the line of my back. I believed she was trying to excite me again.

I yawned and turned over so that I could stare at the stunning vixen who had just given me the best head I had ever experienced. "Nah, Ms. Lady, I gotta get my day goin' in about an hour. Don't even have enough time to get some more sleep."

Chantal frowned. Her expression told me she understood I was telling her to leave.

"We'll do this again," I lied.

Chantal sat still for a minute. She probably thought I would change my mind and tell her to stay.

She must have grasped that I really wanted her to leave, because she climbed out of bed and disappeared into the bathroom. Fifteen minutes later, Chantal stood in the doorway, finally ready to leave.

"Daryl, promise me you'll call," she pleaded with a disappointed look on her face. She leaned into me and reached for a handful of what she had just had in her mouth.

I playfully blocked her. "I will." I kissed her lightly on the lips and pushed her out the door. "Thank God," I said aloud, closing the door behind me and walking over to my bed.

I had to lie to Chantal to get her to leave. I needed to get at least a few more hours of sleep. Even though I enjoyed my night with Chantal, it couldn't become a habit. I was engaged to Briana and I didn't want anyone else getting too attached. I would hit a few ladies here and there, but it was always just sex. Briana was more conservative in the bedroom, and that was exactly how I wanted my future wife. I couldn't imagine her engaging in some of the freakier activities that other women performed on me. I had no desire to witness Briana swallow my semen like Chantal had done. Therefore, until my wedding, I satisfied my lustful appetite with women I didn't care about. Once I say I do, Briana would be the only woman I'd make love to. Briana was the better part of me. She made me want to be the best man I could be. I needed her in my life. Briana was the right to all the wrong I had done and continued to do. In six months, I would make her my wife. It was time for me to get married and have a few kids.

I would be turning twenty-seven the day of our wedding and I wanted to have at least one child before I was thirty. Hopefully, it would be a little boy that I would name Daryl Robert Simms, Jr. Briana and Junior would release the demons that were inside me, the ones that held me captive and forced me to do these detestable things that I knew were wrong. There was no doubt about it—Briana was my angel. She was truly God-sent.

The only time the demons were not tormenting me was when she was near and I looked at her beautiful smile or held her close to me. She was my joy. Loving and naïve, she had no idea of the type of man she was marrying in a few short months.

5

ATLANTA, GA

"Come on, man. Do we really gotta do this now?" My voice rose higher and higher. "It's way too early for the bull. I ain't got time for this." I paced around my hotel room holding my cell phone a few inches from my mouth.

"Jerome, if you would just listen to what I'm saying, I wouldn't have to act like this," the person on the other end of the phone whined. "You know all I wanna do is be with you. I ain't trying to start nothing, baby."

"Yeah, but you always do," I accused. "Just let me call you back." I pressed "end" on my phone before the other person had a chance to respond. Seconds later, my phone was ringing again. I sent the call to voicemail and tossed my cell on the couch. It was five in the morning and I didn't have the energy to argue.

I plopped down on the couch in my deluxe hotel suite beside my continuously ringing phone and dropped my head in my hands. I refused to answer it again and continue with a foolish argument that was only going to upset me more. I was exhausted and already had a dreadful headache. After being up all night and then having to deal with the nonsense early this morning, all I wanted to do was crawl into the bed and go to sleep.

I had been at the Grand Hyatt Atlanta Hotel in Buckhead for a week and still hadn't completed the majority of my tasks. One of the reasons I was behind on my to-do list was because of the caller I had just hung up on. I took a deep breath and tried to forget about the fussing and fighting that had me distracted from my overdue tasks.

The purpose of my visit to Atlanta was for a job interview and to look at some real estate. After living in Charlotte, North Carolina, for the last six years, nothing was left there for me, so it was time to make a move. I had little family in Charlotte, even less friends, and my job wasn't giving me the satisfaction that I needed. It was time for a change and Atlanta would be a great place for a fresh start. I leaned back on the hotel's stiff, plum-colored sofa, put my hands behind my head, and thought of all I had done to get in the predicament that I was in now.

Born and raised in Greensboro, North Carolina, I began to sing at the tender age of eight. I was known at my church and surrounding churches for my powerful voice. Singing became my passion, and even now at thirty-two, I still only felt complete and truly happy when I was belting out my favorite tunes. I adored the town that I grew up in, and after attending a local community college and taking up software development, I was offered my first job at a computer consulting firm. Even though I was working in my career, I still spent a great deal of time traveling to different churches singing and meeting people. I hoped they would assist me in reaching my aspirations of becoming a professional singer. Memories of how young and dumb I was back then filled my mind.

As a twenty-year-old, I received local recognition and praise for my amazing voice, which connected me to many new people and opportunities. After I sang a solo at my church one Sunday for an usher board program, I was approached by the choir director of a visiting church, Vincent Thomas.

Vincent was a tall, slender man with a powerful baritone voice and daunting green eyes. His demeanor made me fear him, but I also wanted to impress him at the same time. Vincent had started his own music group outside of his church. After he heard me sing, he approached me about joining. Once I learned about all the awards that his choir had won in such a short time of being together, I was sold. Convinced that this was the right move for my singing career, I became a part of the group, Vincent Thomas and King's Kingdom. Little did I know, Vincent would open up another world to me.

We spent countless nights together in his studio. One night, after a long session of practicing new songs for an upcoming gospel performance, Vincent changed my life forever. We were sitting beside each other when Vincent stopped the playback of the song that we had just finished working on. I glanced at him and his strong green eyes had an unfamiliar affectionate look to them. His eyes seemed to roam over my lips before he leaned over and planted on me one of the softest kisses I ever had.

"What . . . what did you do that for?" I questioned nervously backing away. The kiss caught me by surprise and I didn't know how to react. I had never been kissed by a man before, and even though I felt I should have punched Vincent dead in his mouth for trying something like that, I honestly didn't want to hurt him.

He rolled his chair closer to mine and grabbed my hands. "Don't be scared, Jerome. I see the look in your eyes. This will just be between us. I can show you things that you never imagined."

The way he held my hands and the calmness in his deep voice relaxed me. He probably observed the unexplained attraction I felt toward him.

It left me utterly confused because I had only been with women and was still very attracted to them. However, this attraction, this desire, could not be controlled. That night, I decided to let it take me into the unknown.

For months after that, Vincent was my teacher and I was his student. He taught me all about the pleasures of being with a man. The sexual episodes that Vincent and I shared were exhilarating, but surprisingly, didn't curve my appetite for women. Thereafter, I lived a double life—I had a girlfriend in public and Vincent in private. My romance with Vincent came to a sudden end after a careless night at my house. I still lived at my parents' home, and after a few drinks, I sneaked Vincent into my room. Usually, our time would be spent at his house so that no one would find out about our secret love affair. That night, I had to be up early in the morning and I declined his invitation to stay at his place. Once we reached my house, the effects of the alcohol had me wanting Vincent more than ever and I persuaded him to come in for a few minutes. We lay in bed under the sheets naked and kissing when my mom walked into the room. I learned later that she had heard noises and came to check on me. I will never forget the look of utter horror and disgust on my mom's face when she saw me in the arms of a man.

Once word got out about my sexual activities, my parents kicked me out and my family disowned me. Since the church family was basically my family, I was also banned from singing at church. I was heartbroken. My cousin, LaToya, lived in Charlotte and convinced me to move after I told her how the family was mistreating me. She allowed me to stay with her for a while until I found a job and got on my feet. My only brother, Omar, even turned his back on me, which hurt worst of all. He was four years younger than me and I had done my best to always look out for him. I was distressed for a while, but with LaToya's help, Charlotte became my home and where I eventually met my fiancée, Tamara.

A relationship with Tamara was my chance to put Vincent behind me and attempt to live life as a straight man. I still had a deep attraction for men, but my love for Tamara was stronger than those desires, or so I thought.

I felt a twinge of remorse when I thought about my sweet and loving Tamara. I tried to love Tamara with all of me and, for the most part, I succeeded in doing that. The part of me that craved a man I suppressed, although ultimately, it got the better of me. The biggest mistake I ever made was to trust someone whom I thought could handle my secret.

LaToya would sometimes visit New Zion Baptist Church with her coworker, Denise. LaToya and Denise invited me to go to church with them one Sunday, and I happily accepted since I missed the spiritual part of my life. Upon entering the mighty doors of New Zion Baptist Church, I was greeted with smiling and friendly faces. Once I heard the amazing choir, and listened to the word from the profound Pastor Simms, I was hooked. I had to be a member of this great church. I joined the following Sunday and felt at home at New Zion. I even became a member of the choir and the lead soloist. I was finally doing what I loved once again. Everything in my life was back on track.

Tamara would finish medical school in Chicago in the fall and soon after, we planned to get married at New Zion. We would start a family immediately after the wedding. If I had kept my urges to myself and not acted on them, I would be four years into my marriage and living in pure bliss, instead of trying to relocate to Atlanta to start a new life once again.

I needed to get my day started, but now that thoughts of New Zion were back, I couldn't get that one person out my head who had played a part in my demise. I kicked the coffee table so hard, it nearly slid across to the other side of the room. Even after all these years, the thought of her made me want to run outside and slam someone's head against a wall.

Her name was Rachel Simms. Rachel was the pastor's daughter and the devil all rolled into one. I remember the first time I saw her. Pastor Simms introduced me to his daughter after I sang my first solo at the church. I tried to maintain my cool, but all I could think of as I watched the sway of her hips when she walked away was how much I wanted to bend her over and feel her wetness dripping down on me. Her honey, caramel skin, flowing black shoulder length hair, and thick sexy body, made my friend in my pants wake up even while standing inside the holy walls. It seemed as if I wasn't the only one that admired her beauty and gawked at her ass as she walked across the church grounds. I noticed that whenever she passed by, every man with half a pulse turned his head. Beauty was definitely her name. Rachel was engaged to be married during the same time I was, which gave me the perfect opening to get close to her. I used the fact that we were both engaged to strike up a conversation every time I saw her. Whenever I talked to Rachel, she was always so stressed out. I played on her vulnerabilities and offered an ear or shoulder to cry on. It was easier than I thought to get her to let down her guard.

I hit the jackpot one day when we were having lunch together. She confided in me about some guy named Terrence that had her second guessing her pending nuptials. She talked about being attracted to him and seeing him on different occasions. Prior to that lunch, I tried to figure out if she was the type of woman who would cheat on her man. I finally got my answer once she started talking about this Terrence guy.

I convinced Rachel to come to my house after we had lunch. She agreed, and I knew I had her right where I wanted her. I intended to seduce her and play out my sexual ambitions with her. Something about Rachel made me desire her more and more each time we talked. Whatever it was, I knew I had to have her.

I left nothing up to chance that night and slipped the date rape drug in her wine when I fixed her a glass. The drug was my guarantee she would be down for what I had planned. We talked for a few hours. The drug seemed to be working because she snuggled up to me on the couch. I kissed her on the forehead and then decided to put my plan into action. It was the perfect time to show her the real reason I invited her over.

In retrospect, I must admit I got a little ahead of myself by arranging the threesome. It would have been wiser for me to get to know Rachel sexually first before including a third person. Instead, because I was really feeling Rachel, I wanted to live out my fantasy before we both got married. With that in mind, I led her to my bedroom and kissed her again with little resistance from her. I opened the door to reveal how the rest of the night would unfold. I didn't foresee that, when she saw Freddie, who I had been sleeping with off and on for a few months, with his legs sprawled open on the bed, she would scream and bolt for the door. I called her continuously that night and begged her to swear to secrecy. Frightened and nervous that she would tell someone, I stayed away from church for a few Sundays. The Sunday I returned, Rachel rededicated her life to God. She announced that she had made mistakes and wanted to live right. I excused myself from the choir and left through the back door. I feared that she would confess in front of the entire church. If her confessions had anything to do with me, I didn't want to be around for the backlash.

I was absent from church a few more Sundays out of humiliation and worry. Upon my return, I assumed that she had disclosed to everyone my secret. All eyes were on me and people were whispering behind my back. Once service concluded, Pastor Simms requested to meet with me.

The same feeling I had when booted out of my family's church in Greensboro came over me and I knew it was time to leave. I didn't go to the meeting and I never returned to New Zion Baptist Church.

I still loathed Rachel for outing me and making me lose my church family. New Zion had become my home, and because of Rachel, all that was gone. My hatred and resentment ultimately caused me to lose Tamara, too. I was so obsessed with Rachel, Tamara told me she felt she couldn't compete. I talked about Rachel all day, but what Tamara thought was a crush was pure malice. I wanted revenge for what she had done to me.

I grabbed the remote off the couch and flipped on the television to the morning news. Rage still coursed through my veins whenever I thought about Rachel. I was not going to rest until she paid for her part in making me lose the two most important things in my life, my fianceé and my church. If it was the last thing I did, no matter how long it took, Rachel would suffer. Vengeance would surely be mine.

6

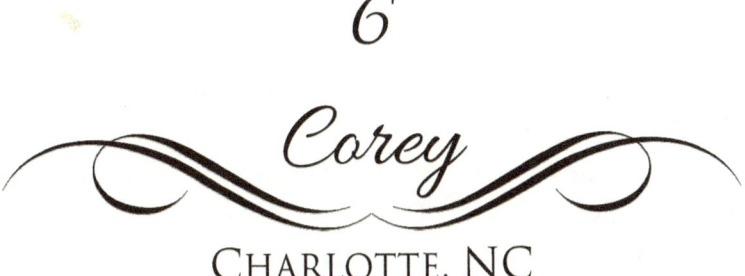

CHARLOTTE, NC

"Yeah right," I taunted. "You know that would mean you actually gotta open your legs and give me some right?" As quickly as those harsh words came out of my mouth, I watched Rachel's mouth drop open. Before she had a chance to respond, I grabbed my keys off the counter and dashed out the door.

"I will be back later," I shouted over my shoulder. I shouldn't have said something so cruel to my wife, but the conversation was going in a direction I didn't want it to. I had to say the most spiteful thing I could imagine to give me an excuse to leave the house.

I jumped into my black Ford Explorer, put the keys in the ignition, and started it. J.Coles's rhythmic voice flowed from my speakers as I glanced at my house before backing out of my driveway.

"I keep my faith strong. I ask the Lord to follow me. I've been unfaithful. I don't know why you call on me."

I was so wrapped up in the relevant lyrics that I didn't pay much attention to my driving. A blazing horn made me slam on the brakes. I looked in my rearview mirror and saw a red Camaro pass by me still blowing the horn as it continued down the street. I looked up and thanked God that I had avoided a foolish accident and damaged my beloved truck.

I remembered the day Rachel and I purchased the truck. Her eyes lit up when she saw it. We had been looking around all day and were both tired. We were at the fifth dealership of the day when I spotted black Thunder sitting on chrome rims in the front row of new trucks. The black 2012 Ford Explorer caught my eye, but as soon as Rachel saw it, she ran up to it and shouted, "Baby, this is it!" Rachel had never acted like that about any vehicle, not even her own cherished white Infiniti. All day, she had been complaining about going home. When I saw her reaction to the Explorer, I knew I had to get it. The welcomed change in her attitude lifted my mood and I fell in love with the truck even more.

Rachel walked around the truck several times with this huge grin on her face. She shook her head a few times, and then asked if we could test drive it. She jumped in like an excited five-year-old, smiling the entire time. At that point, I had no doubts about buying the truck. As I went in with the salesperson to sign the papers, I watched my wife continue to walk around the truck and smile. As I backed my truck up, I thought about how instead of saying those mean things to Rachel to hurt her feelings, it would be good to put that grin on her face again and stop being the cause of her frowns.

"Whad up, cuz!" I walked through Black's door and dapped him up before sitting on his black leather sofa beside his girlfriend, Alisha.

Black's mom and my mom were sisters, but he was more like a brother to me than my first cousin. Over the last few weeks, I found myself at Black's place more often than I was at my own house. Everything I said or did would cause an argument between Rachel and me, so Black's house was my escape.

Black and Alisha lived in a three bedroom apartment on the east side of Charlotte.

They had two kids: a seven-year-old boy, Jeremy, who Alisha had before they met, and a newborn girl, Talia, who they had together. Alisha was the poster child for hood chicks everywhere. I would put money down that Alisha's picture was in the urban dictionary under ghetto girl. She personified ghetto with her prison stance and a blunt hanging out her mouth. Each time I saw her, she wore a weave that looked like someone had spray-painted her hair with five different colors. Today, her long, twenty-two inch hair hung past her shoulders and was bright orange and red. It looked as if wild hot flames were shooting out of the top of Alisha's head. Her hood demeanor complimented Black's street disposition. Black wore thick, long dreads that were halfway down his back and needed attention badly. His new growth was almost half of his dread. Black was super skinny, probably weighed 105 pounds soaking wet, and was as black as hell—hence, his nickname. Black resembled a struggling rapper and Alisha looked like the chick whom he hired off the street to be in his low budget video.

Alisha nodded at me and continued to rock Talia, who was lying on her double D chest. That poor baby was likely being smothered by all her mom's breasts. I watched Talia sleep for a moment, and then turned my head as a queasy feeling erupted in my gut.

"What you smokin on, bruh?" I whispered, not wanting to disturb Talia's nap. I swallowed hard to calm the sick feeling that was going on in my stomach.

At the mention of smoking, Alisha, who was dressed in a pair of red shorts that could pass as underwear and a skimpy, black tank top, picked up the baby and left the room. She returned empty-handed. It was no shock to me that as soon as I referenced smoking, she put Talia down so she could join in. I wouldn't have been surprised if she was high already. Every time I visited them, their apartment smelled like someone had just fired up a blunt.

"What you mean what I'm smokin' on, bruh?" Black laughed, his white t-shirt hanging freely from his thin body. "Man, you ain't smoked wit yo boi in years!"

I looked at Black and shook my head. "Cuz, you don't even know what I been through. I need somethin' right now."

"You ain't said but a word, boi." Black disappeared into his room and walked out holding an already rolled blunt. "It's fiyah, so pace yoself, young'un," he said, lighting it up and passing it to me.

As I put the rolled brown paper to my lips and inhaled the smoke, my mind drifted back to the argument I had with Rachel before I left home. She was having extreme baby fever again.

Every few months, my wife talked about getting off her birth control pills so we could try for a baby. I imagined her logic was that a baby would magically bring us closer to where we used to be. She was ignorant to the fact that a baby was exactly what was tearing us apart. The last thing I wanted to think or talk about was having a child. Just seeing baby Talia before I smoked made me even more anxious to get high and erase the last four years of lies I'd been telling Rachel and myself.

"Man, you gone pass it or just hold it in yo hand," Black asked, snapping me out of my daze. "Puff, puff, pass, homie."

I held the blunt for so long that it went out and had to be relit. I passed it to Black and stared at the television, which was showing the New York Giants playing the San Diego Chargers on Monday Night Football. I wasn't able to watch the Sunday games yesterday, but I wasn't going to miss football again tonight. I deserved it after my long day at work. I also needed a distraction to help me forget the argument that ignited before I left home.

I walked in my house after working twelve hours straight. Before I could get settled, Rachel began her campaign about getting pregnant. It caught me so off guard that, at first, I just looked at her. We had barely touched one another in weeks, and now she wanted to have a baby. I stared at my wife in her oversized sweats, not looking sexy in the least little way.

I said whatever I could think of to start an argument. At the time, all I wanted to do was leave the house. A fight was my ticket out. I had to go before the baby talk continued—before I thought about the child that looked like me, the one I already had.

"You aight, cuz?" Black asked, breaking up my thoughts. "You been in yo own lil' world since you been here."

My focus turned to my cousin and the blunt he was passing me. "Yeah, man, I will be," I answered.

I took another puff just as I heard my phone beeping, which signaled a text message. I looked down at my phone without worrying about Rachel's roaming eyes. It was another picture message. I hadn't looked at the picture messages in the last month. I knew exactly who they were from. It might have been the weed that had me in a trance and made me bold enough to actually look at the message this time.

A lump formed in my throat after I reviewed the picture mail. The subject read, "Hey daddy." My stomach turned into knots as I gazed at a little girl with reddish, brown ponytails, and my face, smiling at me.

7

Von

ATLANTA, GA

*P*ieces of torn paper and busted glass covered my kitchen floor. I rolled off the couch, landing on my hands and knees. I caught a glimpse of the chaos in the kitchen, and it told the story of my previous night. Fragments from the shattered Ciroc bottle made it impossible for me to get a drink of water for my terribly parched mouth. Unable to get off my hands and knees, I crawled over to the kitchen to get a better view of the mess. I didn't remember much from last night. All I could recall was drinking and texting. As usual, I waited for a response that would never come. That probably caused me to smash the bottle. I instantly became frustrated at all the cleaning I would have to do.

It was Tuesday morning and I had called out of work again, the sixth time in the last month. Thankfully, I didn't have to worry about Mercy today, since she was still over at Vivian's house. When I relocated to Atlanta, I rented an apartment until I had Mercy. Once I gave birth and realized how difficult having a newborn was, I ended my lease and moved in with my half-sister.

After staying with Vivian for two years, I desperately needed my own space, so I moved out and got another apartment. My job as a Senior Business Analyst provided me with a great salary of $85,000 a year; therefore, there was no financial reason for me to continue to live with her. The only rationale I had for staying with Vivian so long was that I needed assistance with Mercy.

Even when I moved out, she continued to help me by keeping Mercy two or three times a week.

Although Mercy was a little older and easier to handle now, I still couldn't care for her on my own every day. It wasn't that Mercy was a bad child; she was the complete opposite. My daughter was well-mannered and respectful, thanks to my mom and Vivian's influence. The issue was with me. I had a problem with being responsible for anyone but myself.

I crawled towards the couch again and placed my hands on the cushions to lift myself. I became dizzy and topple over on the couch. I will clean up later, I thought, as I got comfortable and closed my eyes. I had the hardest time sleeping unless I was drunk or high. I tried not to drink too much when Mercy was at home, but as soon as I put her to bed, I found myself taking shots just to forget what I had done years ago. It haunted me every second of the day, but it was worse at night when I was alone. I turned on my side and felt I could be sick at any moment. As I lay very still, waiting for the sick feeling to subside, my mind went to the night

Mercy was conceived. That memory alone usually caused me to be ill. That night nearly four years ago changed my life.

It was a typical weekend. My best friend, Rachel, and I, were supposed to go out and party. She was stressed out about her wedding. Going out was my idea of releasing some of that tension. Most of the time, it would take some major persuasion on my part to get my conservative friend to let her hair down and have some fun. However, in previous weekends, I successfully lured her out of the house and she had the time of her life.

On that fateful Friday night, I called Rachel to ask her to go out. She said she wasn't feeling good. Months later, I found out that she dismissed me to be with my brother-in-law, Terrence. I told her to get some rest. I called another friend who I often hung out with.

Ebony was usually available to party. She was a childhood friend of Rachel and mine and grew up in the same neighborhood as we did. Rachel didn't care for Ebony too much. Ebony was wilder than I was and Rachel complained that when Ebony and I got together, I would get into more trouble than I would get myself into alone. That Friday night, her words proved prophetic.

After we arrived at Crystals, my favorite Reggae club, and visited the bar for a drink, Ebony pulled two white ecstasy pills out of her purse. She popped one of the circular pills in her mouth, chased it with her Crown and Coke, and handed the second one to me.

"Girl, let's have some fun tonight," she said, putting the pill in my hand.

I turned the drug over, and then politely gave it back to my friend. "Nah, chick, you know I just stick to my good smoke. You can have the other stuff."

"I thought you were 'bout that life," Ebony teased. She pushed the pill at me again. Her big brown eyes seemed to beg me to enjoy the drug with her.

"Hunni, you can have that life," I joked, dismissing the pleading in her eyes.

Ebony looked disappointed, but the only drugs that entered my body were alcohol and marijuana. She finally gave up and we hopped on the dance floor, where we spent the remainder of the night. My so-called friend must have dropped the pill in my drink, which probably had something to do with the later events of the night.

When I returned home from the club, I nearly passed out. A knock on the door kept me conscious a little while longer. It was three in the morning, and typically, I would expect one of my male friends to come over. I wasn't prepared for whoever was standing on the other side of that door. Rachel's fiancé, Corey, was in my doorway, and he nearly fell down himself. Since Rachel and I were more like sisters than best friends, I had become just as close to Corey once they began dating. He was like a brother, so it surprised me to see him at my door so late at night.

"Can I come in?" He slurred his words as he leaned against the door with bloodshot eyes. His red dress shirt was untucked from his pants and the top three buttons were loose. I surveyed him from head to toe, and then moved so he could enter my home. He practically stumbled into my apartment. As he did so, he knocked over the bronze lamp in my hallway before he wobbled into the living room and finally fell onto the couch.

"Whoa! Be careful!" I couldn't save my lamp before it crashed to the floor.

"Sorry, Von, but she has really done it now. I mean ain't nothin' ever good enough fo' this chick."

I sat a few inches away from him on the couch, making a conscious effort to translate his slurred language. "It's like she won't let a mug breathe," Corey continued. "Yo, you gotta talk to yo gul. She gettin' on my damn nerves!"

Even though this was not the first time Corey and I had been alone, we had never been by ourselves this late at night. I had been on numerous mall runs with him to pick out birthday, anniversary, and Christmas gifts for Rachel. Just a few months prior, he enlisted me to find out where Rachel wanted to spend their honeymoon. We spent many phone calls going over vacation spots and what my best friend's dream honeymoon would entail.

Tonight felt different. I had never witnessed Corey this drunk before. He was so intoxicated, the way he spoke about Rachel was a complete contrast to the other times he had spoken of her. He always talked about Rachel with loving words. Even when he was frustrated with her, he never spoke that harshly.

It was difficult trying to pay attention to Corey when I was woozy and uncomfortable. I felt very awkward sitting next to him dressed in the tank top and boy shorts that I had changed into as soon as I returned home.

I didn't have the opportunity to change out of my night clothes before Corey arrived and started his tirade about

Rachel. He didn't say anything about my outfit, but I noticed that his eyes kept wandering from my face to my breasts, and then between my legs.

"This wedding 'bout to go down in a few months and I can't deal with her trippin' like this. Make me wanna say forget it!" Corey threw his hands up in the air and one hand landed on my bare leg. Never before had I felt such an intense sensation from a mere touch. I'd heard that the side effects of ecstasy heightened the senses, therefore making me believe that Ebony had indeed slipped me the drug. She confessed days later that she had. However, nothing could have prepared me for the reaction I was having. I glanced at Corey and rested my hand on his.

"Von, man she need to be chill like you," Corey claimed. His lips curled as he continued to talk. "You cool as hell," he said.

Corey's words didn't matter much. My body was on fire and I couldn't comprehend what was happening. Just touching him had me so turned on that I felt like a caged animal longing to be released. My body was screaming. I needed to put this fire out. My panties were soaked and at first, I thought I had pissed in them. Between my legs was throbbing so intensely that I realized it wasn't urine in my underclothes. It was pulsating so much that it literally hurt. I had to end the pain. I stared at Corey but didn't recognize him. He had no face. He had no voice. At that moment, he was just a man that had what I yearned for in his pants.

I remembered kissing him and he began pulling away from me. I snatched at the zipper of his pants. He pushed my hand back, but that didn't stop me.

Somehow I managed to get on my knees in front of him. I pulled at his zipper once again. Finally, I was able to release what I ached for. His long, thick penis sprang forward, enticing me, inviting me to take him into my mouth. I buried my head in his lap and listened to his moans and screams. I glanced up and our eyes met. Suddenly, he grabbed me by my shoulders and slung me off him like I was a rag doll. I hit the floor so hard, I was unable to move.

Corey removed his pants and climbed on top of me. He wrapped his hand around my neck and spread my legs wide. I struggled to loosen his grip from my neck, but my movements only made his hold tighter. He rammed himself into me; his entrance felt like I was being ripped open from the inside out. Corey's quick, piercing plunges back and forth inside me lasted a few minutes, and then ended when he trembled on top of me. It took only a few seconds for him to regain his composure. He then flipped me over and entered me anally. The pain and blood afterwards was what I remembered most. My screams and cries filled the apartment right before I passed out.

The next morning, I woke up naked and alone, still sprawled out on my living room floor. Initially, I thought it was a dream, but once I saw the blood, the bruises, and could hardly walk, I knew it had been a gruesome and real nightmare. It took me forever to get those couple of blood spots out of my carpet. I used everything I could think of to get the stains out. I tried every type of stain remover and cleaner to get my floor clean again. I scrubbed with all that I had inside of me. I cried as I scrubbed. If I could remove the stains, I could erase that night. What did I ever do to Corey to make him savagely violate me in that way? The sex was consensual, but in no way should I have been treated so brutally. The Corey that was at my house that night was not the Corey I had known for years. Those thoughts kept me sick and face down in the toilet the entire day.

I didn't know that that one careless act would produce another human being who would be a constant reminder of what I had done—a permanent sign of the act we had engaged in. Every time I looked at my little girl, who I loved with all of me, I thought about the night I betrayed my best friend.

8

Daryl

ATLANTA, GA

"Hey, beautiful!" I kissed Briana lightly on the cheek and took a seat across from her in the booth. C&B's Grill was a quaint restaurant in the heart of downtown Atlanta. The diner had a small town feel to it and was a favorite of Briana's and mine. C&B's offered a large array of foods, and no matter what our taste buds were craving, C&B's would surely satisfy. We had breakfast at least once a week there. Conflicts often arose in our schedules because I was occupied with the Falcons and Briana was busy with teaching. Today was a teacher's work day, so she didn't have to be at school as early as she did most mornings. It was evident she was thankful for a free morning away from the rowdy first graders she dealt with on a daily basis.

"Hey, baby," Briana sang, her eyes lighting up as she looked at me. Her green blouse matched her greenish, hazel eyes and made her cinnamon-colored skin glow. Briana was part African American and part Caucasian. Her mixed ethnicity blessed her with full pouty lips and a slim, pointed nose. Those characteristics added to the beauty that was my precious Briana Adams. "How was your night, sweetie?"

"Restless, but that's nothing new." I smiled at my fiancée and felt ten times better than I had the night before. Once Chantal left, I tried to go back to sleep but the nightmares continued.

I spent the remainder of the morning watching CNN.

The only time I could sleep was when Briana was beside me. It was yet another reason I had to marry this amazing woman.

Briana flipped her long, sandy hair and gave me her serious motherly face. "Daryl, baby, I think it's time to go to the doctor about your insomnia."

I reached across the table and grabbed Briana's hand. "Babe, I will. Promise. Now, can we eat?"

Briana rolled her eyes and laughed as I motioned for the waitress to come to the table. For the next hour, we discussed our upcoming wedding. Briana was overjoyed about our nuptials and just hearing her ramble on about the wedding delighted me. She was in constant communication with my mother and the plans were coming together nicely. I was grateful that my mom had taken such a liking to Briana. Both my mom and Briana were very special to me. Their growing relationship made me even more ready for our wedding day.

"Oh, sweetie, look at the time!" Briana took one last quick sip of her orange juice and stood to put her jacket on. "I didn't realize it was this late."

"Bri, go head and get to work. I'm gonna stay and finish up my coffee." I stood to give her a kiss before she rushed out the door.

After she left, I thought about all the things I had to do today. Once I finished my coffee, I would head over to the Falcons' training center and get things prepared for the guys to come in within the next hour. Things were going well in my second year as a physical therapist with the Atlanta Falcons. I loved my job and enjoyed helping the guys overcome injuries and get back to the healthy players they needed to be. It gave me great pleasure each time a player would come back to me and tell me how much I had helped them.

I surveyed the restaurant and recognized a few familiar faces. I nodded my head at an older, grey-haired man who seemed to be in the diner every time I came in. A few stools away from him was a gentleman who looked familiar to me. I could only see his profile, but his build and dark skin made me think I knew him. He was dressed in a dark blue suit; perhaps, he was on his way to a business meeting or a job interview. I studied him a little harder, but still couldn't figure out why I recognized him. After a few seconds, he turned around and glanced at me. The stranger hopped off his seat with his coffee mug in hand and approached me.

"Man, don't act like you don't know who I am," he said. He smiled as he place his cup on my table. The strange gentlemen with the light grey eyes stood over me and stuck his hand out.

I grabbed his hand and slowly shook it. I still couldn't figure out who this gentleman was.

"New Zion," the stranger said. The confusion on my face must have been hard to miss. However, once he mentioned my dad's church, I knew exactly who he was.

"Jerome Baxter! Man, it's been a long time! Sit down!" I remembered Jerome from my dad's church, where he used to sing in the choir. He joined the church right before I moved to Atlanta. A few years ago, I had heard he left New Zion, but no one knew why. One minute, he was there, and the next, he was gone without any kind of explanation. My dad told me he had arranged a meeting with Jerome to find out if anything was wrong. Jerome's attendance had dropped, and then he left without ever meeting with my dad. Everyone talked about how odd it was that Jerome had basically disappeared.

He sat down in Briana's seat across from me.

"What'cha doing in the A?" I asked. I thought about asking Jerome about his disappearing act, but decided not to bring that up. I didn't want to make things weird since this was the first time I'd seen him in years.

"I know a few people here, so I come from time to time to get away. I remember hearing that you moved to Atlanta and were working with the Falcons. I never thought I'd run into you. I been thinking about moving, too," Jerome said.

"It was the best move I made. What's keeping you in Charlotte, bruh?"

"Nothing, really." Jerome's phone, which he had placed on the table beside his coffee, beeped. He became distracted. "One sec," he said, frowning as he typed a reply message. He put the phone down and looked at me. "My fiancée and I broke up a while ago, so I've been thinking about moving to see what else is out there," he said.

"Well, this is where I met my fiancée. I'm sure you won't have any problems meeting a new one."

"I have a friend here already. We will see how that works out." Jerome's grey eyes sparkled. His phone beeped again. Jerome sighed and replied to another message.

"Aight, man. I have to go but we should link up sometime. What's yo number, fam?" Jerome asked.

I sipped the last of my coffee and recited my number to Jerome. "Next time you this way, let's hit the bar or something," I suggested.

"That's what's up," Jerome replied. "I gotta make it to a game next time I'm here, too."

"Oh, yeah, we have a nice squad this year. We plan to take it all the way."

"Man, I don't know about all that. You must haven't been paying attention to my Cowboys and my man Dez Bryant. We dem boys!"

I laughed and dapped Jerome up before heading to the counter to pay my ticket. I hadn't planned on staying in the restaurant that long, but it was good running into Jerome.

Just seeing him reminded me of home. There were times I actually missed being there. Then, there were other times that reminded me of the reason I left. Being in my dad's church every Sunday where those moments replayed themselves over and over was far more than I could stand. I only visited home on holidays, and even then, it was a struggle. Home was where I ultimately lost my innocence and changed into a man that I didn't recognize.

9

Rachel

CHARLOTTE, NC

I stared at the computer screen a little too long. All the images and words blurred and my head began to hurt. I wanted to do something to take my mind off the argument that Corey and I had just had. His low blow comment about opening my legs so that we could have a baby only made me want to keep them closed that much more. I wanted so desperately to fill the void that was left from my miscarriage. I felt the only way this could be done was to have another baby. The first time I mentioned it to Corey, I believed he would be on board. I was wrong. For the life of me, I couldn't understand why he became so annoyed. Ever since we started dating, he told me he had always desired to be a father. Now that I wanted to start a family, he would get irate whenever I brought up the subject.

It had been an hour since he left. I sat in front of my computer trying to take my mind off everything we had been going through. My cell phone lay beside the keyboard and I thought about calling Von. We didn't speak as much as we used to and I missed my best friend. I always seemed to catch her at a bad time or when she was drunk, which I couldn't tolerate. Von had always been the carefree one of the two of us. Our friendship began in the sixth grade and she became more a sister to me than a friend.

Despite our closeness, Von had changed a few years back when she got pregnant with my goddaughter, Mercy. She started drinking heavily and appeared to be depressed. I was there for her as much as I could, but my focus was on my marriage. Corey and I had just tied the knot and we were in paradise. Things were great between us. It was probably selfish on my part, but I didn't have time for Von's erratic behavior.

Von confessed that Mercy's father was a guy who she barely knew. She had a one night stand, which didn't surprise me, although she did describe him as tall, handsome, and brown-skinned. I had seen Von with a plethora of different men, and as long as a guy had a penis and money, he was my best friend's type. She even admitted that Mercy's father could have been Corey's twin. My curiosity was piqued, so I asked Von several times to meet her new man. I would have loved to see the man who resembled my husband. Corey was an only child, so he often joked they broke the mold when he was created. My requests to meet Mercy's father were ignored. Von finally explained that it was only a one night stand and the guy didn't want to be a part of Mercy's life. I could not understand how any man wouldn't want to be a part of his child's life. I got the message and dropped the subject of Mercy's father.

I picked up my cell to call Von. The phone rang four times before her voicemail picked up. I ended the call and put the phone down. Then, it chirped, which meant I had a text message. I glanced at my phone and saw that it was from Monica.

"Were you able to help out with that, sis?"

My mind had been so consumed with the argument that I forgot to ask Corey if we could help with Tony's bail. I assumed he was still in jail since she was still asking me for money. I typed a reply

"Sorry, sis, let me check now."

I didn't want to have a conversation with Corey about money. I decided that I would just look at the accounts for myself. This was something I never did since Corey handled paying the bills in the house. We had joint accounts and I had my own personal account. The majority of my money went into our joint account and a small percentage went into my personal account. Corey and I had our accounts set up the same way. At the moment, I only had fifty dollars in my account. I had no recollection of our joint accounts number or password for the online banking application. Corey kept all the important information in his office/man cave downstairs in the basement.

I walked down the creaky steps into his man cave and nearly passed out from the smell of corn chips and beer. I rarely went down there for anything. I certainly never tidied up. Since this was Corey's room, he was responsible for keeping it clean. I could see it was not his top priority. Thirty pairs of Jordans and Nike sneakers were lined up against the walls, creating a rainbow of colors in the dull, white-walled place. The shoes were the only thing that was placed neatly around the room. His dirty clothes were tossed on the frayed, brown sofa and floor. The small trashcan to the right of the couch was overflowing with beer cans and potato chip bags. Corey's Xbox 360 was placed in front of his 50-inch television with his games scattered on the floor next to the console. I was definitely not going to clean up that mess for him. I walked around his games and headed toward his black, metal desk in the corner where his laptop sat. He kept all the official papers, from house documents to job information, in his desk. Somewhere in there had to be our account information. I rummaged through the desk drawer and found various passwords for different applications for his job, codes to the alarm systems in his store, and the security code for the house.

Finally, after ten minutes of searching through papers and folders, I came across the bank information to our joint account. I sat down at his desk and turned on the computer. I logged on and entered the online banking application. Then, I typed in our username and password and waited for the account information to appear. Once it came up on the screen, I saw that we had $200 in the joint account. It was odd there was such a small amount because half of my check had just been deposited into the account two days ago. The mortgage wasn't due until the fifteenth and it was only the first of the month. Maybe Corey paid the bills early, I thought. Even if that was the case, it would have shown where it had been withdrawn from the account.

I trusted Corey to take care of the finances without much input from me. My personal account was enough to meet my feminine needs every month. Money was especially tight since the purchase of our house two years ago. I didn't even ask for new clothes or shoes like I used to when we were dating. I saved my money, and every two or three months, I had a sufficient amount to buy a new dress or some heels that I had been pining over.

I scanned the account history and noticed that, on the first of each month, five hundred dollars was withdrawn. The mortgage was automatically drafted out of our account on the fifteenth. Other bills, such as light, water, cable and even his truck payment, were also drafted from the account and it was listed as such. There was no information about the five hundred dollar withdrawals except the location of the withdrawals. The location was a credit union near uptown Charlotte. I was extremely confused at this point since we didn't even have an account with a credit union and Corey's main office was nowhere near uptown. He had stores all over Charlotte, but headquarters were in the University area of Charlotte.

I had a million questions rushing through my head; however, I wouldn't get any answers without talking to Corey.

I wrote down the account username and password and replaced all of Corey's papers. I didn't want him to think I was snooping around, but I was surely going to ask about the withdrawals every month. Now that I had the account information, I planned to check more often. I didn't want to jump to conclusions too soon. I would simply ask my husband why so much money was being withdrawn out of our account. There had to be a good reason; at least, I hoped there was.

I sent Monica a text to ask her how much she needed. While I waited for her to respond, I logged onto Facebook to take my mind off Corey and the missing money. I scrolled through the news feed. I became bored reviewing my friends' status updates, so I went to the search key and typed in the name Terrence Walker.

I searched his name often. I was never bold enough to friend request him, but just seeing his profile picture made me smile and think of the time we spent together. As I pulled his page up, I noticed that he had changed his profile picture to one where he was standing on a cruise ship. He was smiling and was dressed in a pair of khaki pants and a yellow, short-sleeved shirt that looked amazing against his dark, chocolate skin. I couldn't take my eyes off his picture. The man that I saw in my dreams almost every night was just a keystroke away. I hovered over the "Add Friend" button for a few seconds. Right then, I would have loved to hear Terrence's voice. I hadn't talked to him since before my wedding, but I still remembered his smooth, calming tone.

I used to receive updates on Terrence from Von every so often. Terrence was once married to Von's long, lost half-sister. Von kept me posted on him until he divorced Von's sister a year ago. My affair with Terrence started before I was aware that he was married to Von's sister, Vivian. At the time, Von never knew she had a sister until her dad introduced them. When I learned that her sister was, indeed, Terrence's wife, I was crushed.

It was a very small world. Terrence begged me to wait on him. I told him I couldn't because I didn't believe he'd ever get a divorce. Now that he was available, I was not.

I still hovered over the "add friend" button. I considered reaching out to him many times, but I allowed fear to push the thoughts aside. What if I talked to him and he had completely forgotten about me? I didn't know what kind of reaction I would get from Terrence. I still dreamed about this man. I still felt something whenever I looked at his picture.

I stopped hovering and I finally clicked on the request. The message, "request sent", appeared on the screen. My hands shook. I wasn't sure why I went through with it this time. I viewed his page many times before, and even though I thought about adding him as a friend, I never did. After all that I had experienced with Terrence, once Corey and I made it to the altar, I believed that my life would get back to normal, without all the stress that Corey and I had endured. I know that no life is perfect, but I thought that Corey and I had seen the worst times before walking down the aisle. Constant fights with Corey now made me doubt whether it would really hurt to reach out to Terrence.

I wished for an outlet. I needed someone to talk to. Even though he was the worst person I could possibly choose, I wanted to talk to Terrence more than anyone else. Years ago, I confessed and repented; yet, today, I was miserable. If Terrence could provide some spurts of happiness in my troubled existence, then I was going to push all reason to the side. My husband's belittlement justified my actions. In all honesty, I didn't care very much anymore. I pushed my chair away from the computer and began to pace around my living room. I had no idea if Terrence would accept the request, but only time would tell.

10

Corey

CHARLOTTE, NC

"Will that be all for you today, Mr. Perkins?" the slender, fair-skinned bank teller asked before handing me the deposit slip.

"That's all. Thank you."

This was my routine on the first of the month, every month. I was never late depositing five hundred dollars into Von's account. During my lunch break, I drove to a credit union three miles from the largest Target store in my district. I set up a secret account that only Von and I had access to and made sure that the money was in there for her.

I walked back to my truck, jumped in, and grabbed my phone to send the only text that I would ever send her. "The money is in the account." I didn't change my verbiage or deviate what I said. It was the same exact text I sent at the same time each month. Sometimes, she would respond by cursing me out. Other times, she wouldn't reply at all. Whatever text she sent in response, I never replied. It was hard enough for me to live with the fact that I had a child and was not in her life, but the worst part was that Rachel had no idea that Mercy was mine. I had messed up royally and there was no coming back from it, so I just had to live with this secret. The problems in my marriage were primarily because of this lie. It affected everything in my life, from how I treated my wife to my waning desire to have any more kids.

The guilt ate at me constantly. There were days I couldn't even look at myself in the mirror. The Corey I thought I was would have never conceived a child with his wife's best friend, a child that I couldn't even stand to look at.

I had seen Mercy twice in four years. The first time I laid my eyes on her, she was only three-months-old. Rachel and I traveled to Atlanta to attend a basketball game between the Miami Heat and the Atlanta Hawks. I was hyped by seeing my favorite player, LeBron James, in action. He displayed his "A" game that night on the court, scoring forty-two points and ending the game with a triple double. I cheered until I had no voice left. I had no idea my night would go from great to the absolute worst. After the game, Rachel begged me to stop by Von's house so she could see her goddaughter. The fact that Von agreed to let Rachel be Mercy's godmother disgusted me. Then again, Rachel didn't give Von much of a choice since she designated herself Mercy's godmother without asking.

Rachel called Von as we left the arena. The entire time they talked on the phone, I prayed Von would tell her that she wasn't at home or busy. Rachel, as always, was persistent and didn't give up until Von allowed us to come over. At that moment, the only thing I could think to do was pretend to be sick.

"Baby, I'm not feeling too good. Must've been those nachos," I whined, trying to get Rachel's attention as she talked to Von on the phone.

"Ok, girl, see ya soon!" Rachel squealed before ending the call. She ignored my comment and continued to look down at her phone.

"Did you hear me?" I asked, raising my voice slightly.

Rachel looked at me and rolled her eyes. She still didn't comment or acknowledge my sickness.

I tried again, hoping this time she would believe me.

"I mean, I know you wanna see your girl and her baby, but I really don't feel well. Can we just go home?"

"Ugh," Rachel said, frowning. "Maybe you just have to shit, Corey, dag! Stop acting like a baby!"

Since that didn't work, my next attempt to avoid visiting Von was to start an argument.

"I know you don't give a damn about me. It's always what Rachel wants."

"Take me to Von's house now," Rachel said calmly. She folded her arms across her chest and stared out of the window. No matter what I did, nothing seemed to change Rachel's mind. I was fighting a losing battle; therefore, I gave in and took her to see Von and Mercy.

Von opened the door holding Mercy. I became sick for real. One look at the beautiful, butterscotch-colored little girl, who had my face, and I began heaving violently. Von pointed toward the hall and instructed me that the bathroom was on the left. I took two steps forward and then ran the rest of the way before I vomited in the toilet.

"Girl, he was crying about his stomach all the way here. Hell, I thought he was just lying because he wanted to go home," I heard Rachel tell Von with irritation in her voice.

"Oh," Von replied nonchalantly.

"Hand me my godbaby!" Rachel exclaimed. The entire time that Rachel made goo goo and ga ga noises, everything inside of me ended up in the toilet. After throwing up twice, I returned to the living room and saw Rachel holding Mercy.

"I will be in the car," I mumbled. Rachel was so wrapped up in the baby that she paid me no attention. Von never glanced at me.

She sat motionless as she watched Rachel kiss all over Mercy. It took everything in me not to march across the living room and smack Von. I hated that she even allowed us to come over knowing that I was Mercy's father and we were both lying to Rachel. Instead, I just walked out of the door. I hopped in my truck and wished I had a drink and a cigarette. I was grateful that I didn't have to sit and witness Rachel with Mercy. The hatred of my wife's best friend surely would have become obvious to Rachel if I remained in that apartment.

I despised Von from the moment I met her. Rachel introduced us when Von came to visit her one weekend when Rachel was at Spelman and I was attending Morehouse. Rachel and I had just started dating and I knew immediately I had found something special in my new lady. Von, however, was the complete opposite of Rachel. Von was the typical gold digger who looked for the guys with the most money and flashiest cars. Women like Von always got under my skin. The only difference between Von and the other chicks looking for a come up was that Von was very intelligent and had the ability to make her own money. I couldn't figure out why she succumbed to playing guys and taking what they had when she was clearly on the road to success herself.

The weekend Von came to see Rachel, she was also visiting a few older guys that she knew from Atlanta. She insisted that Rachel accompany her to meet the guys at their apartment. I assumed they must have thought Rachel was as loose as Von, because two of the guys continuously harassed Rachel that night and attempted to take advantage of her. Von was in a room with two other guys. After an hour, Rachel was finally able to get Von out of the room and they left.

Rachel didn't tell me what happened until the next day and I was furious that Von would put her so-called best friend in a situation like that.

Rachel was also very upset, but she eventually forgave Von and they became as close as ever again. To me, Rachel was too good to have a whore as a best friend. From then on, I tolerated Von only to appease Rachel. I tried my best to keep my distance from Von, but time after time, Rachel would put me in situations where I had to deal with her best friend. Rachel loved surprises. For her birthday or any special occasion, instead of just telling me what she wanted, she would direct me to Von for guidance. I ended up spending time and talking to Von more than I cared to.

Once I removed myself from the apartment, after seeing Mercy for the first time, I hoped that my stomach would settle. I waited in the truck for Rachel to finish her visit. As I sat there, I couldn't get the image of Mercy out of my head. She was so innocent and precious. She had no idea what kind of a messed up situation she had entered into. A part of me wanted to protect her while another part wanted to forget she existed. How could something so small and harmless have me so divided? How could a blessing, such as a child, be created in such a horrible way?

The night Mercy was conceived was one I would never forget. I remembered going over to Von's house to see if she could talk some sense into Rachel. To this day, that was my biggest regret. Instead of being at Von's, I should have gone home. Better still, I should have talked to Rachel and not confided in her best friend. Rachel and I had been fighting more than ever over our wedding. I was one argument away from calling the whole thing off. Between Rachel's constant whining and crying, I had no peace. I tried to explain to Rachel that I was dealing with stress on my job, but once Rachel's selfishness kicked in, there was no chance that she'd be concerned about anyone but herself. Von was my last resort. Regardless of the skanky things Von did and how much I disliked her, Rachel seemed to always take her advice.

If I could get Von to talk to Rachel, I knew she would calm down with the wedding craziness. I was so close to being done with Rachel altogether. I needed Von to reason with her best friend.

That night, I had been out with Black at Onyx, a strip club that he practically lived in. We had smoked so many blunts that I lost count. Between the weed and shots of Jameson, I had to wonder how I even made it to Von's apartment. There I was, in the middle of the night, telling my fiancée's best friend that I couldn't handle her anymore. Von wore boy shorts and a tank top, and it was a welcome surprise. She normally dressed in low-cut dresses and things that showed off her curvaceous body; however, I'd never seen her in anything so revealing as what she had on that night. The type of woman Von was turned me off completely, so her skimpy outfits never caught my attention. That night was different. I enjoyed the view of her round ass hanging out of her underwear. Even though I detested Von, I couldn't deny that she was gorgeous and her body would deliver a gay man.

As I explained how I felt to Von, I noticed that she was just as intoxicated as I was. She was higher than I had ever seen her before. She repeated the things I said two and three times, and then would say nothing for a few minutes. She seemed really spaced out. Her eyes darted around the living room as if she was nervous to be sitting next to me. My eyes, however, couldn't stay off of her body. I glanced at the fatness between her thighs as she tucked her gorgeous legs underneath her.

We sat on the couch talking, and before I could react, Von had knelt in front of me and put her head in my lap. I demanded that she get up and pushed her away. No matter how hard I shoved her, she kept coming back.

After I pushed her away the third time, I became weak and gave in. The whole time she had my piece in her mouth, I thought how wrong this was. I thought about how dirty Von was to do this to her best friend's fiancé. She wasn't Rachel's friend at all.

I wanted to leave. I told her no, but I was so aroused by her excessive and intense sucking that I couldn't move. The fact that I was enjoying it made me livid. I wanted to hurt her for putting Rachel in danger and for what she was doing to me. I knew exactly how I would make her feel this pain. If this was what she wanted, then I was going to give it to the tramp in the worst possible way. I found my strength and pushed her head away. She tumbled back on the floor and I jumped on top of her. I was so pissed that using a condom didn't come into my mind. I put my hand around her neck and gave her all the hate and anger I had bottled up inside me. I treated her exactly like I saw her—a nasty trick that deserved to be sexed like one.

An hour later, I left her naked on the floor. Instead of going home, I went to Black's house and stayed over. I woke up the next morning with a migraine. I convinced myself that the previous night had been a bad dream. For two whole days, I made myself believe that it never happened. I didn't see Von again until Rachel miscarried our child.

Once I came face to face with Von at the hospital, I knew indeed that night had taken place. I couldn't even look at her. We took Rachel home and while she slept, Von threatened to tell Rachel about us. So, I confessed to Rachel. It was the watered down version of the truth, but the truth nonetheless. I told her I met a woman that I confided in and we slept together only once. I just didn't tell her that the woman was her best friend.

The day that Von told me she was pregnant was the worst day of my life. Married for three short months, Rachel and I were as happy as hell. We were the couple we had been when we first met. Rachel was even freakier in the bedroom and I couldn't get enough of my wife.

While at work one day, I received a text message from Von asking if we could talk. Von had become distant with

Rachel after the wedding. Rachel confessed that she was so wrapped up in the fact that we were back to the old Corey and Rachel, she didn't pay it much attention.

I called Von and heard the news that changed my life forever. I remember the words like it just happened yesterday.

"Corey, I'm pregnant and it's yours." Von's words were muffled by tears.

"Man, stop playing with me," I shot back, unsure if she was joking or not. If she was, she had to be real sick to even kid about something that serious.

The phone went silent before Von broke out in a loud wail followed by more sobs. "It's true, Corey. It's true."

"I mean, can you take care of it?" I hinted at an abortion.

Still crying, she muttered, "It's too late for that. I am too far along."

"Maybe, it's not mine. Come on, Von. You know your track record with men. How do you even know it's mine?"

The phone went silent again, but this time, Von didn't come back crying. "Oh, it's yours, but just to make sure, I have no problems having a DNA test done."

I was beyond confused, hurt, and scared. Once she mentioned a test, I hung up the phone.

Von kept her word and arranged for me to go to a clinic in Charlotte that would do the testing once Mercy was born. Sure enough, Mercy was 100 percent mine. All I could think about was how hurt Rachel would be. Von promised me that she would take this to her grave, so we set up an account and every month, I deposited money to help take care of Mercy. For the first few years I didn't hear from Von. More recently, she began to send pictures of Mercy and random text messages about how messed up it was that I didn't even ask about Mercy.

To me, Mercy was a mistake, the biggest one I had ever made. I wasn't going to pretend to be the proud father when that was far from the truth. The money was simply to keep Von's mouth shut. The five hundred a month I gave her was one of the reasons money was so tight in my house.

Five hundred bought her silence and gave me a little peace of mind. I put it in the account and sent the text, "Money in the account", every month on the first.

11

Daryl

ATLANTA, GA

Thursday night's game was epic with my Atlanta Falcons beating the Division Rivals, New Orleans Saints, and securing the top seed in the NFC South. I was tired after the game, but I wasn't going to pass up the chance of partying with some of the players and enjoying the Atlanta nightlife. After a Red Bull energy drink, I was ready to see what I could get into. Most of the players were going downtown to a local bar, and then heading over to the strip club, Magic City. Jerome was back in town and had hit me up to see what was happening in Atlanta tonight. To give him a little taste of the nightlife, I invited him to hang with the team. Groupies would surround us, which would give Jerome the chance to see why I loved Atlanta so much.

I sat at the bar talking to Chris, a wide receiver for the team, and drank a Heineken. Then, I spotted Jerome walking into the bar. He was dressed very casually in black slacks and a white button down shirt that displayed his toned arms and abs. The ladies' eyes were on him like he was a superstar who played for the Falcons, too. After tonight, Jerome would be ready to move immediately, I thought as I observed a group of ladies lick their lips when Jerome passed their table. I waved to him and as he approached, I introduced him to my teammate.

"Whad up, folk," Jerome said. He took a seat on the barstool beside me and looked in the direction of the bartender to get a drink.

"Man, I gotta give it to y'all. Y'all played like hell tonight," Jerome said to Chris after ordering a Hennessey and Coke.

As they talked about the game, I admired the view of two ladies standing near the other side of the bar. Briana was in for the night since she had to be up so early for school in the morning. I had already told her good night and I didn't have to worry about her calling me. Jerome and Chris were still talking football, so I decided to send the ladies drinks on me. Both women were extremely sexy. One was a tall, slim, almond-skinned lady with wavy, jet-black hair that reached down her back. Her bronze-colored friend, who was a few inches shorter, rocked a sexy, short, reddish-brown hair cut. I ordered them both a Sex on the Beach mixed drink and asked the waitress to take it to them. In a few minutes, I would introduce myself.

I was about to tell Jerome I was going to meet the women when his phone began to ring. He ignored it the first time. After a few seconds, it began to ring once more.

"I see you got them blowing you up, huh?" I joked, nudging him with my elbow.

He laughed nervously and finished his drink in one gulp. Jerome ordered another shot of Hennessey, but without the coke, then stared at his phone as it began to ring again.

"Aye, man, check out those hunnis over there. I just sent them some drinks and I'm about to go get one. Both are fine, so take your pick."

Jerome glanced at the ladies and then back at his phone.

"Yo, I'm 'bout to take this call real quick." Jerome hopped off the barstool and practically sprinted out the door to answer his phone.

"Ya man should try out for the squad with all that speed he used to run out of here," Chris chuckled.

"That must've been his main lady. Ain't no side chick got you running like that," I said, laughing with Chris. I did think it was somewhat weird how quickly Jerome ran out of the bar. Hopefully, it wasn't anything serious, I thought as I watched him through the glass.

Jerome stood on the corner of the street in front of the bar, talking on his phone and pacing back and forth. He was obviously fighting with someone. Every few seconds, he would throw his hands in the air and shake his head. That woman must really be giving him a hard time, I thought.

I had forgotten all about the ladies that I bought the drinks for until I glanced around the bar and noticed them staring at me.

"Oh, shit, let me go holla at these women," I told Chris before hopping off the barstool and walking toward the ladies. I was on full swag with my red and white checkered buttoned down shirt and black jeans. The ladies wouldn't be able to turn me down even if they wanted to.

I had chatted with the ladies for close to fifteen minutes when Jerome joined us. "Tiffany and Shanice, this is my buddy Jerome," I said, introducing them to Jerome.

"Nice to meet you two beautiful ladies," Jerome said, adjusting the collar on his shirt. "Aye, man. Can I holla at you real quick."

"Excuse us, ladies." We left the two women talking among themselves.

"D, can you take me back to my hotel real quick? Something came up and I have to get back." Jerome's calm disposition had vanished and he was almost frantic now.

"You aight?" I asked, trying to find out what the hell was going on. "Somebody in trouble?"

"Yeah, you can say that," Jerome replied. "I didn't drive here. I was dropped off. I hate to interrupt what you got going on, but you think you can help me out?"

"Man, there will be more groupies later. That's not a big deal." I shrugged, looking back at the ladies. I did want to get Tiffany's number before I left, but maybe I would run into her again. Her short Halle Berry cut complemented her spicy personality and piqued my interest.

"Thanks, man. 'Preciate this," he said before sprinting out the bar again. I watched Jerome as he got back on his phone and started pacing once again down the sidewalk.

I told Chris and the fellas that I would catch up with them later at the strip club. I walked out into the brisk night air and pointed in the direction where my silver Charger was parked. Jerome stayed a few feet behind me still talking on his phone. I didn't want it to be obvious that I was listening to his conversation, but I couldn't help but wonder what had him so uneasy.

"It's not like that. You know what I had going on," he said. I was convinced that his emergency was some woman griping about him being unavailable tonight.

Jerome stayed at a hotel in Buckhead Atlanta about twenty minutes away from the bar. For the entire ride to the hotel, he argued on the phone with the person who was obviously making his night hell. I couldn't hear her, but Jerome's end of the conversation lead me to believe she was very upset that he had gone out tonight.

"Didn't I tell you to chill out," Jerome shouted.

By the time we reached the hotel, the three Heinekens I had were screaming to be released.

"Aye, can I come up and piss real quick?" I asked Jerome. I hoped his company wasn't waiting in his hotel room. I had heard enough on the phone. From the agitated look on Jerome's face, I probably heard more than he wanted me to.

Jerome moved the phone away from his ear and covered it with his hand. "Yeah, my bad about all this, bruh," he whispered.

I parked and followed Jerome to his room on the second floor. Jerome's one bedroom hotel suite was nothing short of amazing. Upon entering, there was a large sitting area occupied by a sofa and loveseat. Beach and sunset paintings and splashes of colors on the walls brought the room to life. I quickly searched Jerome's living quarters and located the bathroom. I ran in to release myself.

I exited the bathroom feeling relieved. I was anxious to get back to the wild night, so I searched for Jerome to tell him

I was leaving. Before I had a chance to call out his name, Jerome walked out of the bedroom still talking on the phone. He had changed out of his jeans and shirt and now wore only basketball shorts. Jerome held up his finger, a signal that he wanted me to wait until he finished his conversation. I hurriedly made my way toward the door. I needed to get out of there as soon as possible. I was very uncomfortable with Jerome's appearance and I didn't want him to notice. Jerome told the person on the phone that he would call later.

"D, thanks again for dropping me off, man. Sorry I had to take you away from the party and pretty ladies." I turned to face Jerome. He smiled, hypnotizing me as I inched closer to the door.

"It's okay, man," I stuttered. "I have to leave." I looked down to avoid staring at his alluring smile.

"You aight, bruh?" Jerome closed the distance between us and stopped when we were inches apart. My hand was on the handle of the door. I had to leave now. I turned the knob as Jerome reached for the door and placed his hand on top of mine.

"You know you don't have to rush off," Jerome whispered in a deep, seductive voice.

He seemed to ignore my nervousness and tightened his grip on my hand so that I couldn't turn the knob. I promptly snatched my hand back and fought the urge to place it on his beautiful, hairless chest.

"I . . . I have people waiting on me," I replied, choking on my words, trying to get myself together.

Jerome winked at me and opened the door. "Aight, bruh, we'll get up later."

It took me a few seconds to move, but once my legs finally listened to my silent commands, I ran out the door towards the elevator. I bolted out of the hotel as if someone was chasing after me. Once I reached my car and sat inside, I took a deep breath and rested my head on the steering wheel. Did Jerome see in me what I tried to hide deep inside? I thought about his mysterious grey eyes and how soft his hand felt on top of mine. His bare, ebony chest and flat, toned abs beckoned me to come closer and caress them. His body called out to me, drawing me in.

"Please God, take away these urges," I cried over and over again. I tried to shake Jerome's image from my head. I needed to erase him from my mental and never think about him again. I removed my hands from the steering wheel and placed them around my body, as if to give myself a hug. I dug my nails into my skin so deep, I drew blood. The pain I inflicted upon myself had to snap me out of fantasizing about Jerome.

For years, I buried this evil spirit and I would not allow Jerome to resurrect it. I had to stay away from him. I had come too far for Jerome to send me down that path again.

12

Jerome

ATLANTA, GA

I was right about Daryl! I was right about him after all! I was so thrilled that I could have danced all over my hotel room. The first time I saw him at C&B's, there was something peculiar about him, but I wasn't quite sure. However, his behavior tonight confirmed that I was correct about Mr. Daryl Simms. I saw it in his eyes and in the way he tensed up when I touched him. He was uneasy when I approached him. We were standing inches apart and it was like he was holding his breath. I took a huge chance making that move. A true heterosexual man might have kicked my ass for touching his hand the way I did. I could have been punched and dragged all over my hotel room. It was risky, but in the end, I am glad I trusted my gut. I had to see if what I believed was really true. Being bisexual for many years, I was extremely good at reading other men. I was a down low brother, which gave me insight and intuition about other down low men. I had a keen sense and could spot them miles away.

Daryl was a strikingly handsome man with his amber tone and lean build. Even though I was highly attracted to him, I didn't want to unleash that side of him for my own sexual satisfaction.

I wanted to maximize the opportunity to get my revenge on Rachel. Rachel had turned down my sexual advances, but her brother definitely would not.

She loved her brother dearly and thought the sun rose and set on his ass. Once his little secret came out, Rachel and her entire family would be destroyed.

A thought hit me suddenly that almost made me lose the joy of my exciting revelation. What if his family already knew about his sexuality and was covering up for him? What if his upcoming wedding was only to hide that he was attracted to men? I thought long and hard about this. How would I create a plan if there were no secrets to disclose?

"Yes!" I screamed, laughing out loud. Even if his family was protecting him, I was certain the church family didn't know. The beloved preacher's son could do no wrong in the eyes of every New Zion member. I would out him just like Rachel had done me. I wasn't sure if she had actually told anyone or not, but the way the church responded to me surely meant something was said. I was convinced enough was revealed that I had to leave New Zion. After I finished with Daryl, he would have to leave, too; he and his entire family, including Rachel. They would feel the pain I had felt for years after being booted from my family's church and also New Zion. I had to devise a way to take them down. This had to be a well thought out and precise plan. I was giddy that I would get to pay back the person that had ended my happiness at New Zion Baptist Church.

I sat on my couch concocting a scheme when my phone rang again. All night, I had been on the phone with Freddie and I was tired of him. I met Freddie years ago at a bar in Charlotte. He was the first guy I was intimate with after moving to the new city. I didn't find out that Freddie knew Rachel from New Zion until after I attempted the threesome.

As I discussed Rachel with Freddie, about how much she intrigued me, he never revealed he knew her or that he'd been run off from the church. He advised me to stay away from her but I thought he was just being jealous.

If I had known they knew each other, I would not have tried the threesome thing. I broke it off with Freddie after that incident, but months later, I started to miss him. Freddie was my little secret that I couldn't shake. I tried to stay away from him, but at times, my body needed him. He knew how weak I was for him and the skills he possessed in the bedroom, so he used them to his advantage. He confided his thoughts that the more he pleased me sexually, the more I'd be willing to do whatever he wanted.

After a couple of months of sneaking around with Freddie again, he announced that he wanted a relationship with me. I was utterly against that. I still loved Tamara and wanted to marry her. Freddie just fulfilled some desires that Tamara couldn't. After Tamara and I became husband and wife, I would permanently end things with Freddie. Unfortunately, because of Rachel, I never made it to the altar with my beloved Tamara.

Freddie and I were involved off and on for five years, and I could honestly say that I had love for him. I cared for Freddie a great deal, but it wasn't enough for me to come out of the closet. I would never live my life as an openly gay man. I still had the dream of having a wife and some kids one day. In my fantasy, though, I would have that and still have Freddie on the side whenever I needed him. It was an unrealistic scenario, but it was my happily ever after.

Freddie relocated to Atlanta a year ago and begged me to make the move as well. I considered it, but I didn't want Freddie to think I was making the move for him. He was rather needy and living in the same city again would mean that he would eventually start his campaign for us to be a couple. Freddie's aggravating calls was the reason my night was ruined. He continually nagged and fussed about seeing me.

He even threatened to come out to the bar and make a scene if I didn't come back to the hotel. Freddie had made good on his threats before, so the best decision was to end my night.

My phone alerted me of a text message. It was almost three in the morning and Freddie was still pissed that I wouldn't allow him to come over. I hit "ignore" on my phone. Seconds later, my phone began to ring. Freddie's phone number appeared on the screen. He required more attention than a woman. I hated when he had his little tantrums, which were increasing as I made plans to move to Atlanta.

I walked to my room still thinking about how Daryl couldn't take his eyes off my chest. The best gift ever practically fell into my lap in the form of Daryl Simms.

13

Von

ATLANTA, GA

*T*he weekend was finally here and I was overjoyed. I was more than ready to let loose and find something to get into. Although I had missed a few days at my job, I was able to make up my work without hearing too much of my boss' mouth. As a consequence, I was only given a warning about my absences. Truthfully, I didn't care much about my job. I really didn't concern myself with a lot anymore, even my daughter.

I attempted to be a better mother to Mercy, although I was well aware that my attempts were weak. If things had been different, I could have been an exceptional mom. If the guilt didn't hold me hostage every day and night, Mercy would have had the mother that she deserved. The shame crippled me. Only alcohol and my medication kept me going.

To get my weekend started, I decided to call Daryl to see what his plans were. Daryl was like a little brother to me since I was so close to Rachel and her family. He moved to Atlanta around the same time I did. I kept my distance from him when Mercy was born because I feared he might see her resemblance to Corey. However, once I started going out again, I ignored my nervousness. The need to have a good time outweighed any worries I had. Daryl was so much fun, and since he worked with the Falcons, he had the best connections.

Daryl introduced me to a few football players whom I briefly dated and provided me with the social life that I so desired. My wildest nights were spent partying with Daryl. One night in particular I would never forget. We attended a party at the home of one of the players on his team. Late in the evening, Daryl approached me with a random woman on his arm and asked if I needed a ride home. I told him that I would find a way home later. He said he didn't want to leave me, but he knew me well—he couldn't force me to go with him. After he left, four football players propositioned me for sex. The six shots of Tequila I had consumed made it easy for me to consent to sleeping with them. I didn't think that men still ran trains on women, but I learned differently. Every part of my body was beyond sore once I returned home.

I didn't completely enjoy the encounter, but during those moments, I felt wanted. I was also distracted from the reality that I had a child by my best friend's husband. For some reason, I felt empowered. I felt like the old Von that would do anything she wanted and was desired by men. I didn't have to think about the daughter who had Corey's face or the payoff I received every month.

I wanted to feel that way again, so I dialed Daryl's number.

"Hey, Von," Daryl answered somberly.

"What's up, D? Something wrong?" Usually when I called, he sounded energetic. Today, he was the complete opposite.

"Nah, just got some stuff on the dome. What's up wit you, sis?"

"Nothing much. Just wanted to know if you knew of any parties going on this weekend. You know I love your fine ass football players," I joked.

"Yeah, sis. Trust me, I know. I haven't heard of anything big happening, but if I do, I'll let you know. I think I'm gonna lay low this weekend."

"You sure you aight?" I didn't like Daryl's tone and became worried about him. He was not sounding like himself at all.

"I'll be ok, Von. I will hit you back later." Daryl hung up the phone before I had a chance to say bye.

Daryl's behavior was really strange. I didn't believe for a second that he was okay. I contemplated calling him again to ask what was going on, but I decided against it. Daryl would never tell anyone if something was bothering him. He always seemed like he could handle everything, no matter what it was. Rachel used to complain all the time about how Daryl meddled in her business and told her what to do, but she could never do the same with him.

I glanced at my cell phone again and suddenly remembered that my mom was coming to town to pick Mercy up for the weekend. I was ecstatic that I didn't have to be responsible for anyone for a few days. I was not that accountable for Mercy during the week, anyway. However, these few days away from Mercy would give me a break from seeing her and the constant reminder her face held. Mercy was in her room taking a nap after being in daycare all day. I hadn't packed anything for her and I was almost certain that all her clothes were dirty. I walked into my kitchen and took a sip from the apple crown royal bottle that was sitting on my counter. I placed it in the cabinet over my stove so that my mom wouldn't see it when she arrived.

As I closed the cabinet, my hands began to shake uncontrollably. Damn, I thought I had this finally under control, I thought as I ran to the bathroom to get my bottle of medicine.

A year ago, after a four-day sabbatical confined to my bed, unable to get up, I went to the doctor and was diagnosed as clinically depressed. The doctor prescribed antidepressants in order to get me functional again.

I didn't take them as much, but every now and then, when the trembling started and I couldn't focus, I needed them. Trying to keep myself from breaking out in tears, which happened every time I felt out of control, I opened the bottle and poured two pills in my hand. I retrieved the crown royal bottle, then downed the pills with one quick swig to the head.

I sat down on the couch and waited for the medicine to kick in. I hoped the medicine would calm me down soon so I would appear relaxed when my mom arrived. The last thing I wanted was for her to lecture me about returning to therapy. I had no desire to sit in a cold, isolated office with someone who didn't know me. I resisted the idea of telling the therapist my darkest secrets while lying on an old, worn out couch where another person had rested their tormented body on just minutes before. Therapy was not for me. I gave it a chance once on the advice of my mother. Telling someone my sins, confessing, and opening up didn't make me feel free. It only made me ponder more about what I had done. After each session, I would drink myself into a stupor and pass out. At my fifth session, I ran out of Dr. Taylor's office, not to return.

My sudden flight from the room was triggered by the discussion about the night of Mercy's conception. Dr. Taylor helped me piece together the parts I couldn't remember.

"Now, Ms. Singler, the night that Corey came over. Do you remember what happened before the encounter?" she asked. She glanced down at her notebook and then up at me.

The frumpy, slender, black lady who appeared to be in her late forties pushed her red-rimmed glasses up on her nose, waiting for my answer.

I turned my head and looked out her office window to avoid any eye contact with her. I shifted on the couch and crossed my ankles. "We were just talking," I said.

She waited a few seconds before asking me her next question. "And how did you feel when you were just talking?"

"I don't know. I was uncomfortable, but I wasn't upset that he was there," I replied, still looking out the window.

"Um hum," Dr. Taylor said as I heard her scribble something down in her notebook. "Von, before the night Mercy was conceived, what did you think of Corey?"

With that question, I turned and stared at the doctor. I cleared my throat. "Honestly, I thought he was one of the best guys I had ever met. He treated Rachel like a queen, when half the time, she was either being selfish or acting like the world revolved around her." As I thought about my friend, I sat up on the couch and placed my hands in my lap. Suddenly, the office became cold, as if someone had turned on the air full blast. I shivered and rubbed my hands together.

"Would Corey have been someone you would have dated, if he wasn't dating your friend?"

I continued to rub my hands together. I knew what Dr. Taylor was trying to get at. "Doc, listen, I didn't want this to happen," I said standing. I felt extremely irritated.

"Wait, Von. I wasn't implying that. Please sit down."

"Rachel didn't know what she had," I continued. "If I had met Corey first, I would have settled down with him and not been out here sleeping with every man that acted like they wanted me."

"Von, please sit down so we can talk about this. You just hit on something very profound. This could be a breakthrough."

Dr. Taylor jumped up from her chair as I darted toward the door. I made a mad dash out of her office, lobby, and building. I didn't stop until I was safely in my car driving home.

I could have blamed the drugs in my system, but deep down inside, I had to wonder if I really wanted to sleep with Corey. Dr. Taylor's questions were digging too deep in places I didn't want to go, places I couldn't go. That session was the last time I would see her.

Dr. Taylor called several times. She wanted to set up another appointment but I never responded to her voicemails. I had no idea how I managed to live with this for four years, but somehow I did, and I had to keep on. Between the alcohol and prescribed medication, I would make it.

I leaped up from the couch after I heard a glass smash.

"Maaaaa, I ain't mean ta dooo it," Mercy wailed before I had a chance to say anything.

I had passed out and fallen into a deep sleep. I forgot that my mom was coming to get Mercy. My daughter must have awaken from her nap, gone into the kitchen, and tried to pour herself some orange juice. The glass container of Tropicana was broken in pieces and Mercy stood barefoot in the middle of the mess. She wore the same orange short sleeved shirt she had worn to daycare, but no pants. She was in her Dora panties and looked frightened at all the glass that surrounded her. I jumped up and ran into the kitchen right before there was a knock at my door. I stepped over the glass and scooped Mercy in my arms.

"Be right there," I yelled, trying to navigate through the broken glass without cutting my foot.

I ran to the door and opened it, with Mercy hanging onto my neck. My mom was on the other side, one hand poised to knock again.

"I thought you weren't here as long as it took you to open the door," my mom said looking me up and down. I adjusted my black skirt and pink blouse so that I looked a little presentable.

"Graaaandma!" Mercy screamed as she jumped out of my arms into my mom's.

"Well, look at my beautiful little Mercy pooh," my mom said. My mom beamed as she gave Mercy a kiss on the cheek. "Where are your pants, lil' lady?"

She walked past me and carried Mercy into the apartment. She placed Mercy on the couch, and then removed her black shawl, which covered a stunning purple and black pants set. My mom was what I had imagined I would be one day. My mother, Mary Singler, was flawless. Her hair was styled in a simple, short haircut and her skin was the same mocha color as mine. She owned her own catering business. I would boast to anyone that my mom could throw down in the kitchen.

She handed me her shawl to hang up and surveyed my apartment before sitting down.

"How is my little butterfly doing," my mom asked, picking up Mercy and placing her on her lap.

Mercy giggled. "I not a budderfly, Grandma. I a little girl."

"You are a little girl who is not speaking correctly," my mom said matter-of-factly. "It is 'I *am* not a *buTTerfly*. I *am* a little girl.' What has your mom been teaching you?"

My mom eyed me and then focused on Mercy as if she was waiting for an answer.

I spoke up before Mercy had a chance to say anything. "Mom, don't start. I am teaching my baby a lot."

"I bet," she replied, not looking at me.

I rolled my eyes at my mom. Mercy was still in her lap as she continued to teach her the correct way to say certain words. My mom and I used to be so close. I missed how we would talk for hours while I helped her prepare for her catering jobs. She constantly hounded me about getting married and having kids. When I told her I was pregnant, she was overjoyed. That excitement left after I told her that Mercy's father didn't want anything to do with her. After I began my downward spiral, things quickly changed between us.

Over the years, my mom's worrying over me transformed into concern for Mercy's well-being. Every other day, my mom called to check on Mercy. After making sure her granddaughter was okay, she would then ask about me.

"Do you have her clothes together, Von?" Mercy was pulling my mom into her bedroom.

"No, ma'am. That's what I was doing when you knocked on the door," I lied.

"Grandmaaaa, come look at my rooooom," Mercy said, still tugging at my mom's arm.

"Ok, baby." My mom glanced at me and then at Mercy. I prepared myself for whatever criticism my mom was about to level at me; instead, she just followed Mercy into her room.

I ran into my laundry room and opened the dryer. Clean clothes had been in there for at least three weeks. I was in the habit of just searching for something to wear in the dryer each morning. The old Von would have never lived like this. Wherever I went, I would always look my best. I thought about all the times Rachel fussed at me for taking so long to get dressed because I had so many clothes that I didn't know what to do with them all. Just as I thought, Mercy had only one clean pair of jeans in the dryer. I wouldn't hear the end of this from my mom. After a few minutes, my mom and Mercy returned to the living room.

Mercy was on her heels and she had put on the jean shorts she had worn earlier. My mom told me not to worry about clothes since she had some at her house. Luck must have really been on my side.

"Be good, baby," I said, bending down to kiss my daughter. Mercy's attention was solely on my mom and I wondered if my child would even miss me. My mom picked up Mercy and carried her to the door.

"We will call you when we make it back to Charlotte," my mom said as she walked down the stairs with Mercy in her arms.

My daughter didn't look back at me. She just held onto her grandmother's neck and smiled as my mom loaded her into the car. As much as I worried that my daughter wouldn't miss me this weekend, I felt a little relief that I would not miss looking at her face and being reminded of Corey, either.

14

Corey

CHARLOTTE, NC

I licked my lips as I gazed at my wife swaying back and forth, singing Beyoncé's song, 7/11, while she helped her mom in the kitchen. She was dressed in a black, fitting, straight dress with a gold chain belt hanging from her waist, and my eyes were glued to her shapely behind. We had just come from church and were over at her folk's house about to have dinner, although my mind was not on the food at the moment. Pastor Simms and I sat in the living room as the remaining two minutes of the Carolina Panthers game played on the television. He watched the game and I watched my wife.

"Run, man, run!" My father-in-law shouted at the Panthers running back, Jonathan Stewart, as he rushed for a first down. "These guys are gonna give me a heart attack," he laughed. "Terrible season, but we still got a chance to make those playoffs. I told Daryl he'd better hope those dirty birds are ready for my Panthers!"

"You right, Pops," I agreed.

I glanced at the television for a split second and then back at my wife. She looked especially beautiful and pleasant today, bouncing around the kitchen, laughing and talking with my mother-in-law and sister-in-law, Monica.

Her attitude was a far change from when she quizzed me about the missing money two weeks ago. I came home and practically was put on the witness stand about the missing five hundred dollars from our account. But ever since that night, Rachel had been happier than she had been in a while. I smiled as I thought about how I was able to make a terrible conversation work to my benefit.

After watching the game at Black's house, I returned home where Rachel bombarded me with questions about the money that I removed from the account every month. Rachel never looked at the finances, so her questions surprised me. For almost four years, I had been taking that money out and she never once checked behind me. Whenever she needed extra money, she would ask me first. Even though things between us had been worse than they had ever been in the last few months, I didn't think that she would look at our account.

At first, I didn't know how to respond. I played dumb and asked her what she was talking about. I knew I had to think of something, so I blurted out the first thing that came to my mind. I debated whether I should turn it back on her and pretend to get upset about her snooping, but Rachel was too smart. She would see right through that.

"You want a child right?" I asked, desperately hoping she would actually believe the lie I was about to tell.

"Don't say it like that Corey. I want us to start a family," Rachel replied.

"It takes money, baby, and I was just putting a little back for that. Half of that is going into another savings account and I'm tryna' pay off a loan with the other half."

I grabbed her hands and guided her to the couch so that we could sit down and talk face to face. I didn't want to start an argument. I wanted her to believe me, so I took the soft approach.

"Baby, I would never hide anything from you. I want us to be prepared when we did decide to have a kid."

"All this time, you been acting like you don't want a family, Corey," Rachel said, lowering her head.

"Rach, you are my family. Wit' all the fussing that we been doing lately, I didn't think it was a good time right now."

She lifted her head and stared at me. "I don't like the arguing either, but things have changed so much. We barely spend time together and it's always about bills and other stuff. We don't have fun like we used to."

"I know, baby," I sighed, relieved that the conversation had moved from the account to spending time together.

I slid closer to my wife and put my arms around her. She looked up at me for a second and then rested her head on my shoulder.

"Let's go to bed, baby," I whispered in her ear. I might have been wrong for lying, but I wasn't going to pass up this chance to turn the argument around and make love to my wife. Nearly a month had passed since we had touched in any way and using my hands to please myself was getting old.

Even Maxine's ghetto ass friends, who were always at her house, started to look good to me.

I reached for Rachel's hand and lead her to the bedroom. The experience we shared in that room was the reason I was staring at my wife now and wishing we were at home rather than her parent's house. Rachel instantly became a beast in the bedroom and reminded me of our first night as husband and wife.

Rachel kissed me so passionately that I had to make sure it was my wife who had her tongue in my mouth. I was used to her wanting foreplay; lately, whenever she gave in to my demands for sex, I had to put in extra work to get her ready. For the last year, Rachel and I had sex once a month; twice, if we weren't mad at each other.

However, that night after our talk, as soon as she threw me on the bed and climbed on top of me, her juices were flowing. As I entered her, she was so soaked that the noises coming from in between her legs were louder than my groans. I was drenched in my wife's wetness and couldn't hold myself back from climaxing. Rachel must have recognized that all too familiar face because she jumped off me and put me in her mouth to catch my release. She didn't miss a drop. Then suprisingly, she looked up at me and swallowed. That was the first time my wife had devoured me in that way and I was shocked and amazed. I tried to get up, but couldn't move. Rachel smiled once again, kissed me on my forehead, and disappeared into the bathroom. I had no idea what had come over her, but for the first time in a long time, I was a satisfied man.

15

Rachel

CHARLOTTE, NC

"Rachel, stop acting like a school girl and hand me that clear dish next to the sink," my mom instructed. "Monica, put a lil' bit of salt in those greens for me, too."

Monica gave me a playful shove, moving me to the right of her, so she could get to the pot on the stove. "Sis, if you smile any harder, I'm gonna start thinkin' you got a piece on the side," she whispered, winking at me. "And I thought you didn't like that song."

I pushed her back gently, laughed, and continued to sing like I was Beyoncé herself.

"Girl, you just came from church. Stop sangin' all that nonsense. And all this dancing you doing now, you need to do at home. You are really putting on the pounds, Rachel." My mom turned around and pointed at my expanding stomach.

I ignored my mom's comment and began to set the table. Even her sarcasm and criticism weren't getting on my nerves today. Nothing could ruin my mood—nothing at all.

"Is Deacon Jeter coming over, Mom?" I asked. I set the extra china plate and utensils on my parent's glass dining room table just in case her answer was yes.

"You know he is. You know that's dad's running partner. Thick as thieves," Monica said, answering for my mom.

"Come over here almost every Sunday and ole' greedy ass be the first one ready to eat." Monica rolled her eyes just as the doorbell rang. "Wonder who that could be?" she quipped.

"Girl, stop that!" My mom swatted at Monica, but missed, and only hit air. "Take your slick mouth in there and open the door. It's the Lord's Day and you are using language like that in our house!"

"Mom, I'm sorry, but you do realize I am grown now?" Monica laughed, walking out of the kitchen to answer the door.

As I put the finishing touches on the table, I glanced at Corey sitting in the living room with my dad watching football. The relaxed look that was plastered on Corey's face was indeed thanks to me, but my permanent smile had come from another source. My happiness came from another place that I had no choice but to keep to myself.

For the last two weeks, Terrence and I had been in constant communication every day. It was as if we hadn't missed a beat within the last four years. The night I was going to talk to Corey about the missing money, Terrence accepted my friend request. Once my phone notified me that he had accepted, I threw my phone on the couch and rushed over to my computer to log into Facebook to get a better look at his profile. My hands trembled as I clicked on his name and his page popped up. I gazed at his picture—he was just as gorgeous as I remembered. I scrolled down his time line and saw a few statuses here and there, and pictures of his kids and him at different events. I was engrossed in his page when an instant message box popped up at the bottom of my screen. Oh, my God, it was a message from Terrence. My heart stopped and I held my breath as I clicked on the message.

Terrence: Well, well, well. Have I died and gone to heaven?

I laughed out loud and thought about all the things that I could to say to Terrence. There was no way I could tell him everything that I wanted to. I still couldn't believe that I was actually about to talk to him.

Rachel: If you are in heaven, I must be dreaming.

Terrence: LOL! How have you been, Ms. Rachel?? I was so shocked to see your friend request.

Rachel: I am good! I happened to run up on your page and thought I would reach out. It has been so long . . .

Terrence: Indeed it has been a long time. But no matter how long, you will never be forgotten.

My heart raced so much, I couldn't think of a reply. Did he really just say he would never forget me? I felt the same exact way, but should I tell him that?

Rachel: I will never forget you either.

I replied before I had a chance to think about what I typed. I thought back to the times that we spent together and how, at one time, this man had me open like the Grand Canyon. The memories of the secret getaways and talks instantly aroused me. It was always so intense with him whenever we made love.

Terrence: So how is married life, Mrs. Perkins?

As soon as I crafted a response to his question in my head, I heard Corey outside. I left my computer and peeked out the window to see Corey's Ford Explorer. It was the same truck that Terrence had and the only reason I wanted Corey to buy it. It reminded me of Terrence every time I rode in it. For some reason, it made me feel close to him. I ran back over to the computer and typed Terrence a message.

Rachel: I have to go but is it okay if I hit you back later?

Terrence: Sure beautiful . . . I will be waiting.

I had to hide the smile that was now frozen on my face when Corey walked in the door. There was still the discussion of the misplaced funds that had to take place.

Corey staggered in the house and one look told me that he had been drinking at Black's house. I hated Black and his dumb, ghetto broad, Alisha. Alisha and I had absolutely nothing in common, but Corey forced all of us to hang out together from time to time. Whenever we went out with them, I stayed on my phone texting or playing games. I am sure she thought I was anti-social, but what were we going to talk about? Where she bought her colorful weave? How many blunts she smoked that day? I was thankful that I hadn't seen her or Black in a while and hopefully, it would stay that way.

Once Corey became comfortable, I just jumped into the conversation. The only way to tackle this issue was to just ask. I prepared myself for Corey's defensive attitude. Surprisingly, instead of evading my questions, he told me that he wanted to save money to have a child. I was totally shocked by his answer since every time I brought up the subject of a child, he became upset. The conversation was going better than expected and I didn't want to ruin it by acting as if I didn't believe Corey, especially since I was still trying to hide the excitement from talking to Terrence.

After we talked, I made love to Corey better than I had in at least a year. I felt a little guilty closing my eyes and imagining Terrence in the bed with me instead of Corey, but from Corey's moans and screams, he didn't notice anything different. Once I put Corey to sleep, I practically leaped out of the bed so that I could log back onto Facebook. It was almost one o'clock in the morning and I wasn't sure if Terrence would be online to receive my message.

I found Terrence's name on my friend list, and sure enough, there was a green circle next to it indicating that he was online. I took a deep breath and quickly typed hello. In a matter of seconds, I received a response.

Terrence: Was just thinking about you.

Rachel: Oh really? And what were you thinking about?

Terrence: The night that I held you for the first time. Do you remember that?

Rachel: How could I ever forget?

Terrence: Those thoughts made me smile days when I didn't think I could.

I leaned back in my chair and thought about all the conversations and experiences Terrence and I had shared in the past.

Terrence: Is it too late to call? I just want to hear your voice.

I debated whether to take Terrence's call. It would be too risky with Corey in the bedroom.

Rachel: Tomorrow

For the next two hours, my face was inches away from the computer screen, engaged in an online conversation with Terrence. I literally floated as I caught up with him. After so many nights dreaming about him, I was finally communicating with him again. I pinched myself several times to make sure I wasn't just lying on the couch like always and fantasizing about him. No, this wasn't a dream; I really was talking to Terrence. Hours passed and we didn't want to end the conversation. I saw double and fought sleep like a new born baby. I reluctantly told Terrence good bye and that I would talk to him tomorrow. That night, as I slept on my couch, I had the biggest smile glued on my face. I had just talked to the man that would soon appear in my dreams and no words could explain the joy that I felt.

16

Daryl

ATLANTA, GA

*V*on called me all weekend looking for parties. Even though I loved her like a big sister, she got on my nerves. I had more important things to deal with besides keeping her updated on the latest events around Atlanta. I was supposed to call her back the previous night, but I was too distracted to talk.

Back in the day, I used to have the biggest crush on my sister's best friend. All my friends wanted her, too. She was beyond gorgeous with a body that deserved to be praised. When I was younger, I would get embarrassed every time she came around. The blood would always rush to my pants and I would stand there trying to hide a woody. That's just how bad Von was. However, all that had changed. She was still pretty, but not as irresistible as she once was. She didn't carry herself like she once did. The one word I always thought of when I talked to Von was "thirsty". Thirsty meant she chased after a good time or a man. I don't know what happened to her, but after she had Mercy, she just fell off.

Nevertheless, that didn't stop my teammates from treating her like all the other groupies they ran through. She seemed drawn to that lifestyle.

I ignored her all weekend, and since it was Sunday, I thought I'd give her a call. I reached for my phone, and as I was about to dial Von's number, my parents' picture popped up.

"Hello," I answered.

"Hey, honey, how are you?" My mom's voice sang over the phone.

Relieved that it was her and not my dad, I let out a sigh and fell back on my couch. I loved both my parents dearly, but I wasn't in the mood to talk to my dad. The conversations with my father always dealt with me being the best man I could be, which included being strong, taking care of everyone, and knowing my role both as a man and the head of the household. He was a lot tougher on me than my sisters. While I understood his reasoning for that, I didn't need to hear all the time about the many responsibilities I had. There was no time for feelings in my conversations with my dad. Men weren't supposed to display those types of emotions. We were supposed to be firm and be able to handle everything, no matter what. My dad and I had our moments where we enjoyed a football or basketball game together, but they were few and far in between.

Growing up, I rarely saw him at home. He was always at the church or a church event. Those were the times I really needed my dad. Those were the times I would cry out for him, but he wasn't there. He mentioned to everyone else how close we were, but that was far from the truth, in my eyes. My dad didn't know me. All he knew was the son he wanted me to be, the son that everyone depended on. But if everyone was depending on me, who would I depend on? That's where my mom came in. I had a very special place in my heart for my mom. She was the person I went to when everything around me was falling apart. She never judged me and was always there. My mom and I had a bond that no one could destroy.

"I'm okay, Mom," I said.

"Baby, you don't sound too okay. What's going on? You and Briana good?"

My sister, Rachel, complained endlessly about how our mom meddled in her life, but I appreciated the concern. I was just fine having my mom in my business.

"Yeah, Mom, we're good. I'm just under a lot of stress. Trying to maintain and stay focused."

"Don't let stress send you to an early grave, honey. Is there anything you need me to do? I spoke to Briana and things for the wedding are coming along nicely. You know, I am an old pro at this now," she chuckled. Her laugh lightened my mood.

"Yeah, I know," I said, smiling. After all my mom went through with my sister's wedding a few years ago, my wedding should seem like a breeze.

"Okay, Daryl, let me know if you need anything at all. Like y'all kids say, I got ya back, baby." My mom laughed again. I laughed with her this time and told her that I love her.

"I love you too, sugar," she said right before she hung up the phone.

If anyone could make me feel better, it was my mom. I could remember the many nights I called her at two, three, or four in the morning when my nightmares would get the best of me. Once my dad was asleep, he was in a coma, and I didn't have to worry about waking him with my late night calls. My mom would get up and talk to me until I calmed down and was able to go to sleep. Contrary to popular belief, I was truly a momma's boy. To the public and to my dad, I was the smaller version of him, definitely Pastor Simms' son.

As I grew up, I did everything I could to make my dad proud. During those times I felt alone or that I wasn't good enough for my dad, my mom cheered me on and built me up. She would never let anyone hurt me and could even sense when I was in danger. My mom was my heart.

After talking with her, I felt so much better that I decided not to call Von. I would text her later to make sure she was okay. Allowing Jerome to see how he affected me was a mistake, but I knew exactly how to handle the situation. I would just stay away from him. I had no other choice.

My job had me constantly in contact with football players and other men of authority. For years, no one got to me the way Jerome had. I was always around half naked men and never did my head turn. I truly thought that I was finally cured from those spirits; however, the incident with Jerome showed me clearly that I was wrong. No matter what I felt, though, I could not allow this to take over my life. I was almost at the altar with Briana and I would not let anyone mess that up for me. My mom felt the same way, and her reassurances that things would go smoothly on my wedding day was all I needed to hear. My wedding day and birthday would be the best time of my life. I couldn't wait for the celebration. All I had to do was put everything else behind me.

My phone was still in my hand. Searching though my contacts, I came upon Jerome's number. Before I could give it a second thought, I deleted his contact information. I refused to allow those demons to come back when I had fought so hard to free myself of them. They would not control me again. I was looking toward the future from now on.

17

Jerome

ATLANTA, GA

"I enjoyed you too, babe," I replied, ironing my shirt for a second interview at a small software company downtown.

"Will I see you again tonight?" Freddie's voice came across my speaker phone.

"Maybe."

"What does maybe mean, Jerome?" Freddie whined.

Here we go again, I thought as I put on my freshly-ironed, blue, dress shirt. I unplugged the iron and picked up the phone.

"It just means that I have a long day and I'll let you know if we can get up later."

Freddie spent the night with me and I had given him the time and attention he had been crying for all week. That still seemed like it wasn't enough for him. He was worse than a female with all his neediness and mood swings.

"Romie, you know I wish we could be together every night," Freddie purred.

I walked in the bathroom and glanced at myself in the mirror. I rubbed my face and traced my goatee, which was lined perfectly, with my fingers.

"If I get this job, we will be able to see each other more." I wasn't going to give in to Freddie's behavior today. "Now, I have to go so I won't be late for my interview."

"Good luck. Call me later, baby, okay?"

"Aight," I replied, still staring at myself in the mirror. I hated that my eyes looked a little puffy and red, but I couldn't dwell on that.

I was exhausted after a long night with Freddie, but I still had to pull myself together for this interview. This was the second interview with this company and if everything went well today, I believed they would offer me the job. Visine would just have to be the cure for my eyes.

Atlanta really appealed to me and I was all set to make the move if I was granted a job offer. Thriftiness was a strong trait of mine, which provided me a good cushion as far as my savings; however, living in that hotel nearly ate all of it. If I needed anything, Freddie was more than willing to help, but I would never get to the point of asking him for assistance. Dependency would definitely send the wrong message since he desired a relationship with me. My dealings with Freddie had carried on far longer than they should have, anyway. I had every intention of ending things with him a year ago when I realized he was becoming serious. However, the things he did in bed persuaded me to keep things going with him.

Even though Freddie and I were involved, I still loved women. I just had an appetite for men as well. I continued to date women and a few of them wanted to get serious. They had no idea that I was bisexual and I didn't deem it necessary to disclose those details. I wasn't ashamed of my attraction to men, but I didn't want to deal with the fall out of telling someone that. It was another reason that being with Freddie was a tad risky. He had threatened to tell my secret so many times that I had to play damage control many nights. Whenever he thought I was dating someone else, he would have a tantrum and totally flip out.

I recalled the time I came home after a date with a beautiful, super model type chick.

After dinner and a movie, we came back to my hotel room and were greeted by a message Freddie had taped to my door. I read the note and was immediately pissed off. Freddie had threatened to be there in fifteen minutes if I let her come in. The last thing I wanted was for him to cause a scene and out me to my date. I politely told her that the note was about an emergency and I would need to take her home. I wasn't surprised to see Freddie's car parked outside when I returned to the hotel.

I walked to my room and saw Freddie posted beside my door with his arms folded across his chest.

"Had fun on your lil' date?" Freddie asked. "You know better than to bring that skinny slut back here." Freddie smiled as if he had control of the situation.

I glared at Freddie. I was so furious at him for making me end my date that I wanted to shake him.

"You think this is funny?" I shot at him. I lowered my voice so no one else could hear me. Two ladies passed by us. I waited until they got on the elevator before I finished my conversation.

"I let this go on for way too long," I continued. "I'm done dude. I don't have to answer to you or no one else. Go home, Freddie. We are over."

Between my putting the key in the door and opening it, Freddie's hands found my pants zipper. In one flash, my pants were around my ankles and Freddie was on his knees. Scared that someone would see us in the hallway; I opened the door and pushed him inside. Needless to say, I couldn't end things that night. He knew my weakness and he knew exactly what to do to curb my anger.

Freddie was beside himself when I informed him about my second interview with the company and if offered the job, I would make the move to Atlanta. I never told him that I was a hundred percent sure about the move until last night when he stayed over. What I had planned for Daryl made it clear that Atlanta was where I needed to be.

The interview went extremely well and I was informally granted the job right there in the office, but because of formalities, I would have to wait for the official offer. As I ate lunch in the hotel restaurant, I received a call from Mr. Burgess, my soon-to-be manager, who offered me the software developer position at the Canton Software Group. I was overjoyed to accept the job and the $95,000 salary that accompanied the offer. Barely able to contain myself, I called my cousin, Latoya, and left her a voicemail that I was finally making the move. The next person I wanted to share my great news with was Daryl. I hadn't talked to or seen Daryl since the night he ran out of my hotel room. I didn't want to come off too pushy and scare him away, so I decided to take the subtle route. This job offer presented me the perfect chance to hit up Daryl and tell him about my new opportunity.

I dialed his number and after getting his voicemail, I decided to text him the good news.

> Hey man, just wanted to share my good news. Got the job and will be moving to the A. We should get some drinks to celebrate.

I waited a few minutes to see if he would respond. The restaurant began to fill up with the lunch crowd rolling in. It was a little after noon when I glanced at my phone again, hoping that Daryl would reply. Twenty minutes had passed and my phone sat on the table silent.

I sipped on my water, waiting and hoping for a text back. Still nothing. Well, no need for me to sit down here and wait, I thought, as I prepared to go to my room. As I retrieved my jacket from the back of my chair, a smooth voice startled me from behind.

"I thought you wanted to celebrate."

It took me only seconds to recognize that sexy voice. I turned around and was face to face with Daryl. Dressed in a pair of khaki pants and a canary yellow shirt, his lean, muscular build almost made me put my arms around him right there in the middle of the restaurant.

"I have some drinks in my room if you want to join me." I restrained myself and gave him my killer smile instead, which was known to make the ladies and men weak.

Daryl hesitated for a moment and then gestured toward the restaurant doors. "Lead the way," he said, finally smiling.

Bingo! I thought to myself as I made my way to my room with Daryl following closely on my heels.

18

Von

ATLANTA, GA

aryl didn't call me back, but that wasn't going to stop me from finding something or someone to do Saturday night. I called John, one of the football players from Daryl's team I still communicated with from time to time. John, along with a few other guys, had planned to visit a new club downtown and invited me to meet them there. I had to put myself together for the night, so I had my hair, nails, and feet done. For a moment, I felt like the old Von again. The Von that could get anyone she wanted. The Von that ran Charlotte and didn't care about the consequences. The Von that hurt men instead of getting hurt. I twirled around and smiled at myself in the full length mirror that hung from the closet in my bedroom. Placing both of my hands on the small of my back, I arched my back and admired the way my breasts almost popped out of the low-cut, black, body con dress. The push-up bra really worked miracles.

"Bish, tonight is our night!" I said aloud, giving myself a pep talk. "Let's show them how Von used to do!"

Sunday morning came too quickly and I was still very intoxicated. I attempted to drive to my apartment from DeWayne's hotel suite at the Four Seasons.

DeWayne Gordan was the fastest running back on the Atlanta Falcons. I had chased him for months and all my flirting finally paid off. I grabbed my sunglasses from the console, then smiled as the evening replayed in my mind. I drove my silver Yukon onto I-285 for the quickest route home. I pulled down my sun visor before putting my glasses on, and glanced at myself in the mirror. My hair was sweated out and matted to my head and there were only a few traces of makeup left. Makeup surely would have helped the bags under my eyes, I thought. Disgusted by the image that stared back at me, I flipped up my visor and looked out my rearview mirror. I placed my sunglasses on my face, turned the volume up on my radio, and began to sing along with Fetty Wap about being a Trap Queen.

As I coasted along the Interstate, DeWayne crossed my mind. He was one of the guys who was in John's company. I saw him from time to time when I was with Daryl; however, he would only greet me and engaged in no further conversation. At the club, I had the perfect opportunity to make small talk because he actually paid me some attention. I flirted with him all night and he finally invited me back to his hotel. I was prepared to see what this handsome, brown-skinned brother with the sexiest beard I had ever seen, could do.

When I walked into the room, I was disappointed to find two ladies already waiting for him in bed. Realizing that this may be the only time I could be with DeWayne, I ignored the disheartening feeling and joined them in bed. That was my first time being with three people at once and I had to sniff a line of coke to really become comfortable with so many hands on my body. Once the drugs took over, my body was a plain canvas as the other two women and DeWayne used all their sexual appendages to paint and create a picture of sex. The next few hours consisted of arms, legs, licking, sticking, and cum everywhere.

I was so engrossed in my memories that I didn't see the black BMW switch lanes in front of me and stop abruptly. I swerved toward the outside lane to avoid direct impact with the car and slammed on the brakes.

"Shit!" I yelled as I threw up my hands at the guy in the Beemer in front of me. If I hadn't looked at the road when I did, I would have hit him in the back. I placed both hands on the steering wheel for a second and regained my composure. Traffic was at a complete stand still. It was odd for the interstate to be so backed up on a Sunday morning. Unless there was a game or another event going on, traffic was usually pretty smooth on Sundays. The Falcons had a bye week, a week when they didn't have a scheduled game, so the other thing that could be holding up traffic was an accident.

Traffic began to move at a snail's pace as I came upon what had caused the slowdown. To my right and two lanes over was a silver Yukon that probably once looked exactly like mine. The front bumper of the truck was smashed in almost all the way to the windshield. The sides were also mashed in. In front and behind the truck were two other cars that were destroyed as well. Seeing that Yukon made me queasy. It resembled my truck so much that I couldn't stop looking at it. Blaring horns snapped me out of my daze but not my disbelief at how mangled the truck was.

"I hope everyone is ok," I whispered.

Once I got home and took a much needed bath, I climbed in bed to try to get a few more hours of sleep before Mercy came home. My phone lay beside me. I heard the quick beep signaling that I had a text message.

At first, I wasn't going to look. After seeing that Yukon on the side of the road, completely demolished, I didn't feel like talking to anyone. The sight of that truck made me realize how reckless I had been over the past few months. As much as I had been drinking and driving, I could have easily been in such a horrific accident.

I stirred in bed trying to get comfortable. My phone beeped with another text message. Maybe it was DeWayne telling me that he wanted to see me again, I thought. I grabbed my phone and typed in my code to unlock it. The two text messages upset me so badly, my worry and concern over the truck accident were replaced by pure hate.

After all these years, I couldn't believe he actually sent me a message. After all the ignored texts and pictures, he wanted to talk. I blinked a few times and then rubbed my eyes to make sure the messages really existed. A second look confirmed that the two text messages were still there.

"Hey, u busy?" read the first message. The second one that followed two minutes later read, "Can we talk?"

I wasn't sure if I was angry that he had the audacity to text me now, or just mad that he had ignored me for so long. Either way, Corey Perkins would have to wait. Because he had ignored my texts, I would do the same to him. I was curious, though, about what he wanted to discuss. However, my spiteful side wanted to give him a taste of his own medicine. I threw my phone on the bed and turned on my side to get some rest before my daughter returned.

19

CHARLOTTE, NC

I turned my head and watched two ladies pass by my car in the garage. I sat in my car for nearly an hour and did not want to go home. I didn't feel like being around Corey, but more importantly, I didn't want to end the conversation that I was having. The air in my car was blasting so hard, it blew my hair across my face. I turned it down on low and sank back into the driver's seat, waiting on him to come back to the phone.

A feeling of déjà vu came over me. My stomach did the same flips they had done years ago. I couldn't forget about those wretched butterflies. They invaded and were creating havoc once again.

"Sorry, about that. You still there?"

"I am not going anywhere," I said. I was smiling so hard that my cheeks began to hurt.

"Uh huh, I heard that from you before," he laughed.

I groaned. "Don't remind me, please."

"Well, believe me, if I ever get you again, I'm putting up a fight before I let you go."

"You tried to do that before, Terrence. Now that you brought that up, what happened at the end? What was up with all those threats?" I referred to the threats Terrence made a few weeks before my wedding when I told him that we shouldn't see each other anymore.

I traveled to Atlanta for a visit and to tell him about the child that I had miscarried. His child. I had only planned to talk, but we made love again after I told him about Corey's unfaithfulness.

I left feeling confused and was almost in an awful accident on my way home. I knew I had to end things then. However, Terrence did not take the news well. I shared with him that we'd lost a child and it sent him over the edge. He threatened to tell Corey about us if I didn't call off my wedding. Terrence pleaded with me to wait until he was able to get out of his marriage. At that time, I thought that I was supposed to be with Corey. Now, I wasn't so sure.

"Rachel, I wanted you to be mine. Sorry about the threats." Terrence sighed. "After the wedding, I wanted to reach out so many times and apologize. You know I would have never hurt you."

"I know." I paused for a second before asking my next question. Even though the conversation had flowed without any uncomfortable silences for the last hour, I was still unsure about asking him a question that I had harbored for the last few years.

Terrence probably sensed my hesitation. "Rachel?" he asked.

Before I lost the nerve, I asked quickly, "Were you at my wedding, Terrence?" A few seconds of silence passed and I began to wonder if he was still there.

"Hello?" I said.

"Rach, I just wanted to see you," Terrence confessed. "I had to see you and how you looked in your dress. I imagined it was me up there and not Corey."

"So, you were there?" My eyes watered up as I thought back to the reception. I thought I had seen him but I wasn't sure.

"Just for a little while at the reception. I had to see you. I'm sorry."

I took a deep breath. He really had loved me. He loved me enough to be there on my wedding day.

"No need to apologize. Part of me wishes you were still acting crazy and had stopped the wedding."

"You don't mean that," Terrence said.

"Yes, I do," I replied softly.

I had filled Terrence in on everything that was going on between Corey and me, including the recent discovery of the five hundred dollars Corey had been saving each month. Terrence listened like always and offered no advice, except for me to keep my eyes opened. I asked his opinion whether he thought that Corey was lying. He didn't respond and just repeated that I should pay attention.

"You know, I have been sitting in this car for an hour, right?"

Terrence laughed. "Well, I'm still in my office. It's been pretty hard to focus ever since I received that friend request."

I laughed along with Terrence and thought about how I was so glad that I had finally mustered the courage to send it.

"Do you think we can see one another?" Terrence asked.

I closed my eyes and laid my head on the headrest. Simply talking to Terrence was opening a forbidden door. Even if the door was open, did it mean I had to walk all the way through? Could I just peek in and play with the idea of him and me? Even though I was tempted, I had learned my lesson years ago and was not going to make the same mistakes.

"I think we should keep it like this for a while." I probably should have told Terrence that we didn't need to see each other at all, but I didn't want to close that door completely.

"For now," Terrence replied. "I have kept you on the phone long enough, sweetheart. Go home and text me when you get there."

"Ok," I said with the same jaw cracking smile on my face.

I reached my house and texted Terrence to let him know I made it safely. He quickly responded that he was glad and enjoyed talking to me. It was almost seven and Corey hadn't arrived at home yet. He would either text or call and let me know he would be home shortly or it was going to be a late night for him at the store. Hoping the latter, I decided to get dinner started.

As I fried the pork chops, Terrence and I texted back and forth. I was so giddy. I ran from the stove to my phone, which was charging on the kitchen bar, to make sure I didn't burn the food. In the middle of a text that I was sending to Terrence, to tell him how silly he was, Corey's face popped up. It was going on eight now. That meant he had another long night ahead of him.

"Hey, babe." I answered the phone singing. I was also dancing, too.

"Hey, what are you doing?" Corey huffed. I could tell that he was either tired or aggravated.

"Cooking us some food," I chirped.

"Cool. Well leave me a plate in the microwave. It's gonna be a long night."

"I figured that, and it's cool."

"It is?" Corey quizzed. "You sho'?"

"Yeah, baby, handle your business. Your food will be waiting when you get here."

"Um, ok, baby. I love you."

"Love you, too," I replied, blowing Corey a kiss through the phone.

Corey was maybe questioning my saying it was cool for him to stay late. He also probably expected me to complain like always. Corey and I were still getting along fairly well, so there was no reason to get mad. In all honesty, Corey's late night allowed me more time to talk to Terrence. As soon as I hung up with Corey, I called Terrence instead of sending him a text.

I turned the stove on low and plopped down in Corey's recliner, ready to enjoy the hours of conversation that I knew was about to take place. That Cheshire cat smile was permanently fixed on my face for now.

20

Corey

CHARLOTTE, NC

t least one thing was going right for me, I thought, as I hung up the phone with Rachel. Thankfully, I didn't have to hear her mouth about my work schedule. Even though things had been pretty easy for me at home lately, I didn't want to get too comfortable and think Rachel would be okay with me continuously working late. For now, she seemed as if she wasn't bothered by my schedule and that was just fine with me. It would probably be midnight before I made it home anyway. I was exhausted, but inventory was being done at all stores. I had to make trips to at least three in my district to make sure they were accounting for everything. I dreaded inventory time, but unfortunately, it was a necessary evil in the retail industry.

I wiped the sweat from my forehead and glanced around the stockroom at all the boxes that needed to be counted. This was going to be a long night.

"Aye, Mo, grab that box in the corner and start scanning those items," I hollered across the room at the Assistant Manager, Maurice.

"Aight," he called back before disappearing behind the packed shelves. There was no way we were going to get all of this counted by midnight, but midnight was my cut off point.

Planted on a footstool, I was deep into scanning when one of the associates who worked the floor rushed into the stockroom. Maxine called out Mo's name twice without a response from him. When she walked around the corner, I spotted her.

"Corey, you know where Mo is?" Maxine asked, walking back and forth trying to locate him.

I looked at Maxine and noticed how her Target uniform hugged her ass, making it look like she had two ripe melons following her. My eyes roamed her body as she inspected the room searching for Mo.

"I think he was over there, behind those shelves," I said, pointing toward the area where I had last seen Mo.

"Okay, thanks," Maxine said, switching off towards the shelves. My eyes followed her hips as they disappeared to the back. Maxine was a beautiful, copper-colored woman in her mid-thirties, working part-time so that she could make sure her kids had everything they wanted for Christmas. She was a single mother of two and very strong and independent. We would talk often whenever I needed to check on this store. I tried to hide my attraction, but today, seeing her butt bounce in those fitted khakis pants, I couldn't help but stare. I thought about doing some innocent flirting with her, but then I realized I was thinking with the head in my pants and not the one on my shoulders. It had been a little over the month since Rachel questioned me about the money and things were slowly getting back to normal. Unfortunately, normal between my wife and me included having no sex and arguing. We only fussed every so often; but the fire that had ignited the night of the money discussion, and a few weeks after, was gradually burning out.

I shouldn't complain, since I was getting a little more sex than I had been getting in months, but I could tell it wasn't going to last much longer. That was likely the reason my mouth was practically watering when I looked at Maxine.

I was in a daze thinking of a plan to romance my wife in order to get another passionate night like the one we had weeks ago, when I felt my phone vibrating in my pocket. I grabbed it and saw Von's number lighting up the screen. Two days had passed since I asked Von to call me. The fact that she was just now getting back to me was probably done out of spite. After four years of ignoring her texts and pictures, I had finally texted her. The only reason I wanted to talk was to see if we could agree to a smaller payment each month. I felt terrible lying to Rachel about the money. I had nothing in savings to back up the lie I'd told her. My plan was to give Von three hundred instead of five each month and save the rest. Hopefully, if Rachel ever wanted to see how much I had saved, there would at least be something there.

Von made great money working at the corporate offices of a bank, so I prayed that she wouldn't make a big deal about the two hundred dollar reduction. I honestly didn't want to talk to her. I had managed to avoid, all these years, having to talk about the mistake we made. Every time I thought about Von and Mercy, I would get this deep, sick, erupting feeling in the pit of my stomach. Undeniably, that was my guilt, but with every passing year, the pain didn't ease up like I had hoped it would. It never left.

Rather than listen to Von's voice, I decided to send her a reply text. The shorter the text, the better.

"Hey, I am going to have to cut the money back to 300 instead of 500 a month. Rachel looked at the accounts and I had to lie and say I was saving money. It will still be deposited on the first."

The best approach would be to tell her what I was going to do rather than ask. That way, she would have no choice but to go along with what I said. I wasn't asking for permission. I was informing her how things were going to be.

I waited ten minutes for her response, but got nothing. I placed the phone on the box of scarves that I had been counting and picked up the scanner off the floor. As I began to use it, my phone rang again. Von's number reappeared on the screen. Normally, I would have let it go to voicemail, but I thought about the lie that I had told Rachel. I needed to cover my tracks.

"Hello," I shouted in the phone. I didn't intend to raise my voice, but the stockroom was much louder with two more associates helping with inventory.

At first, I didn't hear anything but silence on the phone.

Getting aggravated, I said louder, "Hello?"

Still nothing. I was about to hang up when I heard a soft voice whisper, "Hello."

A lump formed in my throat and my face turned red. I gripped my phone tighter. I prayed that Von hadn't done what I thought she did.

"Hello," the small voice repeated.

I swallowed hard and tried to catch my breath. I hadn't heard Mercy's voice in years. The last time I heard that small, delicate voice was two years ago when I walked in the room and Rachel was talking to her on the phone.

I tried to get myself together so that I could speak but nothing came out. I cleared my throat several times before I was able to say anything. "P-p-put your mom on the phone," I whispered.

"Okay," Mercy said. "Maaaa, somebody on da phone," I heard her call out.

"Yes?" Von asked smugly after a few seconds.

"I can't believe you just did that!" I growled. "Why would you put her on the phone?"

"Oh, you didn't want to talk to your daughter, Corey? The one you haven't seen or talked to in years. You do know you have a daughter, right?" Von taunted.

"Listen, Von." I lowered my voice. "I just wanted to let you know about the money, that's all. I don't need anything extra."

"You have made it painfully clear that you don't want anything more from us. I go through the same thing with the guilt, but I still acknowledge that she is here. You can't even do that, Corey?"

"She wasn't supposed to be here . . . ."

"Go to hell, Corey! It happened and she is here! My baby is not a mistake," Von screamed. "Oh, and that three hundred dollars is not enough. I think it's time to take this to court."

My heart began to race. "You would do that to Rachel?" I nervously asked.

A cold, calculating laugh traveled from the other end of the phone. "No, but I would do that to you."

Before I had a chance to respond, Von hung up.

I looked at the phone for a second not believing what I had just heard. I dialed Von's number. No answer. I tried five more times and she still would not answer.

Would she really take me to court and take the chance of Rachel finding out about Mercy? About what happened that night? I wasn't in Mercy's life, but I paid her every month. What more did she want? In my eyes, Mercy was a mistake. A night that should have never happened.

My chest began to tighten as I thought about the hurt that Rachel would feel if she found out. My marriage wouldn't survive this. Von couldn't do this to me. I had been staring at the floor for five minutes when I heard Mo approach me.

"You aight, Corey?"

I finally looked up from the spot I had been glaring at.

"Nah, man. I need to leave for a minute. Can you hold it down until I get back?"

"Sure, Dave is coming in, so we will have some extra help." Mo was referring to the manager of the store.

I jumped up, grabbed my keys out of the office, and ran out of the store. "Damn Von and inventory!" I said, guiding my truck in the direction of Black's house.

21

Daryl

ATLANTA, GA

"Pray, baby, pray," my mom urged through the phone. Even though we were miles apart, I could almost feel the holy oil that I knew she had in her hand. After last night, I needed to douse myself a few times in the Godly liquid.

I didn't tell my mother what happened, but the connection and bond we shared was so strong, she told me she called to see if I was all right. It was after midnight, and before my mom called, I was sitting in the darkness of my townhome after having another sexual encounter with Jerome. Even though I deleted his number, once he sent a text informing me of his move to Atlanta, I couldn't resist the urge to join him in his hotel room. That one episode led to many more over the past few weeks. I was on my couch with my left hand wrapped around the black handle of my silver, loaded Glock, and in my right hand was a picture of me at the age of six. In the photo, I was smiling with not a care in the world. My mom had dressed me in a red baseball hat that was too small for my head, and matching red shorts and a blue shirt. The picture screamed that fashion was not a priority for my parents. I turned the photo over and looked at the handwritten date on the back. It was taken years before I changed, which was the reason I always kept it with me. It was when I was still innocent. When I still felt free. I turned the picture over and stared at the little boy, who, in return stared at me.

"Don't ever grow up," I whispered to my six-year-old self.

Tears streamed down my face. I placed the picture next to me on the couch and turned my attention to the gun. The steel was cold and heavy. I had to use extra strength just to hold it steady. I rubbed my finger over the rough grooves in the handle. The silver sides of the pistol shone so clearly that I could see my reflection. The reflection of a lost soul. It had been a while since I had taken the gun out of its home at the top of my bedroom closet. I felt safe with it in my house. Even though I didn't live in the crime infested parts of Atlanta, there were robberies every blue moon in the communities that surrounded mine.

The remnants of last night stirred around in my head.

"Damn demons!" I shouted through tears as I thought about the demons that overtook my body and made me have sex with Jerome in his hotel room.

Five years had passed since I succumbed to my hidden desires of being with a man. The last time I was with a man was my last year of college. That was one of the reasons I moved to Atlanta. I wanted to leave that behind me. Being with a man was against everything that I was raised to believe and I hated that part of me. I loathed that, at times, I longed for a man's touch. I despised that I wanted a man to kiss me. I hated it so much that I wanted to kill that part of me. And if that meant killing all of me, so be it. I raised the gun and pressed it against my chest. It weighed even more now that I was weakened by my tears. Then, I changed my mind and placed the loaded gun against my temple. If I was going to do this, then I had to do it right. I wanted to eliminate any chance of living through this. If I survived, the part of me that craved men lived, too. I took a few deep breathes to prepare myself to pull the trigger.

I thought I'd set my phone to vibrate, so it surprised me when I heard it ring. I ignored it at first.

After a few seconds of the continuous ringing, I glanced down to see my mom's smiling face displayed. I had to take her call even if I didn't want to talk to anyone at the moment. If I ignored her, she would just continue to call back until I finally answered. Briana had called an hour earlier and I didn't take her call. I always answer her, no matter what. My mom was different, though. She could feel when something was wrong with me. I needed her more now than ever, and deep down inside, I felt she knew that.

After we talked for an hour, she began to pray. My mom was deep in prayer, commanding the devil away and asking God to place his hands on me.

"My precious Lord, we cast the devil away. He has no power over your children. We praise your holy name. Whatever my son is going through, wrap your loving arms around him. Satan, you will not win!" My mom continued to pray. "No matter what stress or worry that has a hold on

Daryl free him, Lord. Let him accept that he is not perfect and does not have to be."

My mom wasn't aware of my desires but she knew that something was not right. She figured my stress was stemming from me trying to be perfect for my dad. She thought I was scared that I wouldn't be able to live up to what he wanted me to be. To be without flaws in the eyes of Pastor Robert Simms was an impossible task—one that I tried to fulfill every day.

Her prayers were helping, and in the middle of my mom's pleading to God, I placed the gun on the coffee table in front of me. The desire to kill that ugly part of me was gone for now. I didn't know if it would come back, but I would have to deal with what I had done and try to move on.

My mom's prayers had turned to singing. She belted out "Something About The Name Jesus." I joined her on the second verse as my silent tears gained a voice and became sobs. When I felt this low, my mom wouldn't ask for blow by blow details but would just pray for me.

I loved my mom with everything in me and she had no idea how many times she had saved me from myself, just like tonight.

"I love you so much, mom," I mumbled after we finished singing the last verse.

"Baby, let's talk some more," my mom suggested. Apparently, she didn't want to end our conversation. "We can sing another song."

"Mom, I promise, I'm okay now. Get some rest."

"I love you, son. I will call you in the morning."

I hung up the phone and wiped my wet face. I carried the gun back to its home. The weight didn't have much effect on me anymore as I placed it in the box. I turned around and glanced at my bed. It reminded me so much of the bed I had laid across the previous night. My body intertwined with Jerome's, kissing and touching like we were both starving for one another.

I shook my head and began to hum the song that my mom and I had just sang together. I knew I wouldn't get much sleep tonight. Between thoughts of my encounter with Jerome and my never ending nightmare, sleep was nowhere in sight.

I walked into the kitchen and reached for the Ciroc bottle that was on top of my refrigerator. I searched my cabinet for a shot glass. I couldn't find one, so I twisted the top off the bottle, put it to my mouth, and turned it up.

Two deep gulps later and I felt a little more relaxed as I walked back to the living room. My picture still sat in the same spot as before. I tossed the picture on the coffee table, plopped down on the couch with the bottle in my hand and closed my eyes. If I couldn't naturally fall asleep, then I would make myself pass out, I thought. I turned up the bottle once again, making sure I didn't waste one drop.

22

Rachel

CHARLOTTE, NC

I expected at any moment to wake up in my living room. I imagined that I would jump up at any second and pray that Corey didn't hear me whispering Terrence's name. I assumed that I would be sitting on my couch in the middle of the night thinking about how I just saw Terrence once again in my dreams. But this time I didn't have to wake up. This time I didn't have to peep around the corner of my bedroom door to make sure Corey didn't hear me talking in my sleep. No, I didn't need to do any of that because the man who was constantly on my mind and in my dreams was now sitting across the table from me. I wasn't asleep or daydreaming. I was wide awake staring at Mr. Terrence Walker.

The breathtaking man who I had not seen in over four years was inches away from me with the biggest smile I had ever seen spread across his handsome face. My heart fluttered and felt like it would burst with delight when I laid my eyes on Terrence. He was divine. His physique proved that the past four years had been amazing to him. Everything was wonderful, from his toned and fit frame to his ravishing, dark chocolate skin and his radiant smile. When he hugged me, I became weak and fell into his arms. He wrapped those magnificent chiseled arms around me and held me close. So close that his cologne was now mine.

His scent was on my skin and I never wanted to wash it off. I needed to hold onto any and everything that I could of this fantastic man. I never thought the day would ever come that I would be face to face with the man that I wished had become my husband.

Terrence placed his coffee mug on the table and winked at me. "Cat got your tongue now?" He smiled that same smile that I used to love so much.

I didn't know how to answer the question he had asked, so I just sat there and glanced out the window. We had been sitting in a new trendy sports bar in uptown Charlotte for the last hour. SportsOne's atmosphere was laid back, but at the same time, encompassed the glitzy scene that uptown possessed. Since I had visited the bar on one occasion before, I thought it would be a perfect place to meet Terrence.

I finally gave in to meeting with him after a month of phone conversations. Truthfully, I wanted to see him long before now, but fear always made me say no whenever he asked for an in person visit.

Terrence cocked his head to the side and repeated his question. "Where do you want this to go, Rachel?"

"I don't know. It took a lot for me to see you." I sipped a little of my lemon drop martini before putting the slender glass on the table. It was early afternoon, and normally, I wouldn't drink so soon in the day, but I needed something to get me through this meeting with the man who had once stolen my heart.

He reached across the table and grabbed my hand. "I don't believe in coincidences and things just happening. We came in contact again for a reason. To this day, I've never felt about anyone the way I felt and still feel for you."

His hand was warm and I didn't want to let it go. I grinned and looked down at our hands, intertwined, like we belonged to one another.

"It's funny how the tables have turned, huh?" I laughed.

"Yeah, but some things never change, like the fact that I'm sure and you are still not. This might sound crazy, but four years didn't make me love you any less. Married or not, I am not giving up on you Rachel, on us . . . ."

"How can you be so sure?" I asked.

"Some things you don't have to sit there and wonder about. We analyze and overthink so much these days," Terrence said. "Sometimes, you just have to follow your heart. Rachel, my heart never left yours."

I didn't say anything. I just looked at Terrence and wished I didn't have to leave him. It was Saturday afternoon and Corey would be working all day. I didn't run the risk of Corey asking where I was, but I didn't want to stay out for too long.

As if he had read my mind, he said exactly what I was thinking. "It took me four years to see you again and I don't want to leave you."

"I promise it won't be the last time, Terrence."

I wasn't sure about the questions he was asking, but I was positive that I would see him again. There was no way, after all these years, this would be the one and only time I laid my eyes on the piece of heaven before me.

"Good, then I will wait patiently until the next time, Ms. Rachel." Terrence walked around the table and assisted me out of my seat like he had done so many years ago. Taking my hand, he led me out of the bar towards Corey's truck.

That morning, I'd asked Corey if he could get the oil changed in my car and leave me his truck in case I needed to go somewhere. He didn't mind, which surprised me because he loved driving his truck. I had noticed that, ever since I found the accounts and missing money, he had lost the attitude that was a trait of his.

When I arrived at SportsOne, Terrence was already sitting inside. He didn't get a chance to see what I was driving. As we walked out of the bar, I pressed the button on my key ring to unlock the truck and waited on Terrence's reaction to the vehicle.

"I see you have good taste." Terrence chuckled. "Is this yours?"

I smiled. "It's Corey's. When we were out shopping, I saw this truck and immediately thought of you. I always feel close to you when I am in it."

"You can be close to me anytime you want now," Terrence said as he pulled me into him. I couldn't resist and didn't try. He placed a soft kiss on my lips that sent chills throughout my body. I opened my mouth slightly and allowed his tongue to ease its way inside for a second. Not wanting to get too deep, I pulled back. I ended the kiss that I had dreamed about for so long. I placed my thumb on Terrence's lips and rubbed the pink lipstick that was now stained on his mouth.

He stopped me by gently grabbing my hand and putting my thumb in his mouth. He closed his eyes and slowly sucked on my thumb and then each of my fingers. I was getting caught up in the moment and didn't want to leave him, but I knew it was time to go. I pulled my finger from his mouth and placed another light kiss on his lips.

"You still taste just like I remember," Terrence whispered, pulling me in for another hug. His arms felt just like I had remembered. I breathed in his scent and closed my eyes.

The four years of being apart were a distant memory, and even though things had changed, still some remained the same.

On my way home, I listened to K. Michelle singing about her wishes to build a man.

However, I didn't need to build one. I had just left the man that would be perfect for me. Sadly, I didn't see that until it was too late. Terrence looked extremely handsome in his dark blue slacks and tangerine colored shirt. The bright color looked incredible against his dark skin. And that bald head! I missed rubbing that beautiful, bald head immensely. Memories of the last time I caressed Terrence's head were interrupted by my ringing phone.

"Hey, D!" I crooned into the phone. Daryl hadn't called me all week and that was not like him. He was always calling to check on me, especially since Corey and I were having problems. Even though he was close to Corey, Daryl was my brother and was always there for me. He was the strongest guy I knew. He was younger than Monica and me, but he acted as if we were his baby sisters. He had always been over protective of us since we were kids. Daryl was so much like my dad that I often called him my second father.

"Hey, baby girl, how is everything going?" His voice sounded weird and he cleared his throat several times.

"Everything is everything," I teased. "What's up with you? Why haven't I heard from you all week?"

"Just been going through some thangs, Rach. But you know me, I'll be just fine."

"You know I'm here, baby bro." I called Daryl baby brother whenever I wanted to help him. He was always available to help me.

"Aight, enough with that baby bro mess. I'm grown and I'll be okay. I just wanted to make sure my sister was good." His voice was clear and stern now. He hated when I referred to him as my baby brother.

"Yes, D," I sighed. "I'm great, no worries."

"Aight then. Tell Corey to hit me up later, sis. Love you."

"I love you too, D." I ended the call but I was still worried about my brother. Something about his voice didn't sound right. He would never tell me if anything was wrong, even if it was serious. He wanted everyone to believe that nothing ever bothered him. The only person that he would let in at times was my meddling mother. Their bond was different than hers with Monica and me. She was closer to

Daryl and I always wondered why. Maybe it had something to do with his being the only boy and the fact that my dad expected so much from him. I hoped he really was okay, I thought, as I threw my phone onto the passenger side seat and allowed K. Michelle to sing me the rest of the way home.

23

ATLANTA, GA

I rushed into the living room and snatched my phone away from Freddie. "What the hell!" I shouted, stuffing the phone in my pants pocket and getting in Freddie's face. Of all the little games that Freddie played, he knew better than to invade my privacy by looking through my phone. My fists were balled up and I felt like punching Freddie dead in his mouth.

He jumped up from the couch and started to back away, putting a good distance between us. He stumbled over the rug and caught his balance on the dining table chair. He moved the chair in front of him to keep it between us.

"Man, why the hell are you in my phone?" I shouted again. Freddie wasn't speaking and I was ready to wrap my hands around his puny neck.

Freddie put his arms in front of him for protection and continued to back up into the kitchen. "Hold on babe, hold on," he quickly replied.

"Ain't no hold on, Freddie! You have no right to go through my stuff!"

Freddie stopped moving and stood his ground. "You getting all swole on me, but answer this. Why are you texting Daryl Simms? And naked pictures of you, at that! Daryl is not gay!"

I stopped in mid-stride and glowered at Freddie. I was seeing red and wanting nothing more than to hit Freddie so that he would stop talking.

"That has nothing to do with you," I growled.

"If you are screwing me, then it does," Freddie said. He rolled his neck as I thought about breaking it.

There was no way I wanted Freddie finding out about Daryl. I couldn't believe I had been so careless as to leave my phone lying near Freddie when I went to the bathroom. Before I went to the bathroom, I was sitting on the couch in my hotel suite with Freddie in front of me. He was on his knees giving me head and I had just released. I excused myself to go to the bathroom. When I came back, I saw Freddie with my phone in his hands going through my messages. During the entire course of our relationship, he never touched my phone, at least not to my knowledge. I wasn't sure what had provoked his curiosity this time.

"How about I just call Daryl myself," Freddie said, mocking me. "I have the number now."

"No!" I shouted, startling Freddie. Being mad and threatening Freddie wasn't working so I decided to try something else.

"Baby, listen. It's nothing like that," I said calmly. "Come over here and sit down so we can talk." I pointed toward the couch.

Freddie didn't budge at first, but after I sat down and loosened my jeans to expose myself, he lapped over like a lost puppy. After he sat down, he placed his head in my lap and started round two of his favorite things to do for me.

I had to make him forget about Daryl and what he saw in my phone. The last thing I needed was for Freddie to get involved and mess up my revenge on Rachel. I was also becoming fond of Daryl.

It wasn't in my plan to fall for him, but having him in my room the last few nights was more than I had ever expected. I was looking forward to many more times with Mr. Daryl Simms.

I glanced down at the top of Freddie's bald head and rubbed it.

"You don't have to worry about anyone," I whispered tilting my head back and closing my eyes.

Since I was trying to keep Freddie quiet about the text messages in my phone, I decided to allow him to spend the night at my hotel room. I didn't make that a habit. I didn't want him thinking that we were a couple, but tonight, I had to stop him from being mad at me and asking more questions about Daryl. Spending the night seemed to calm him down. After he woke up, we went another round in the bedroom and he didn't have any more to say about Daryl Simms. He couldn't have known this would be the last time he lay his head on my pillow for the night. Things between Freddie and me had to be over. Freddie looking through my phone was the last straw. I had come too far with my plan of getting revenge on Rachel. Freddie's nonsense would surely cause all my hard work to be in vain.

To put icing on the cake and make sure he kept his mouth shut, I made Freddie breakfast. I had to make sure we were all the way good before ending things. How I was going to end things, I really didn't know, but it had to be in a way that he wouldn't hate me, if that was possible. Maybe if I saw something just as incriminating in his phone, I could use that against him to break things off.

As Freddie slept, I left breakfast cooking in the kitchen and I tiptoed into the bedroom. I took Freddie's phone from the nightstand by the bed.

Freddie was a hard sleeper so I wasn't concerned too much with waking him. I waited until I walked back in the kitchen to look through his phone. I saw text messages to five different guys describing their sexual escapades. Nude pictures appeared everywhere in his messages. I was pleased that I had so much to use to end things with Freddie. I had everything I needed, but before I placed his phone back on the nightstand, I decided to glance at his call log.

I clicked on the recently dialed numbers, and once I saw the last person Freddie had called, it felt like someone had just sucker punched me in the gut. The last number dialed on Freddie's phone at 9:55 pm, right before I caught him with my phone, was that of Pastor Robert Simms.

24

Von

ATLANTA, GA

Corey had the nerve to think that he could cut the money he sent for Mercy every month and I was just supposed to go along with it. That was the least he could do and now, he didn't even want to do that. To me, it wasn't even about the money. I made enough money on my job to take care of both Mercy and me. The money that Corey gave me each month was put into a savings account for Mercy. It was the principle of it all and the reason why I put Mercy on the phone. He was going to acknowledge her if it was the last thing he did. I was the only one living day by day with the guilt of betraying my best friend. Corey still had Rachel and the life that he always wanted with her.

I used to think that Corey was the perfect man, so caring and loving. I had to admit to myself that I was jealous of the relationship that Rachel and Corey had. She would piss me off to no end when she would complain about him, especially while they were planning their wedding. Every day, she would whine about Corey. Every day, she would cry that he didn't pay her enough attention. She fussed about Corey not being there for her all the time. Rachel was beyond selfish and I told her that many times. Perhaps that's why I initiated sex with Corey that night. I could blame it on the drugs as much as I wanted, but maybe, deep down inside, I wanted that to happen.

Corey was the type of guy that I could have settled down with. Rachel had what every woman longed for in a man and still found the need to complain. I was jealous and wanted him. I could have made him a lot happier than Rachel.

Contrary to popular belief, Rachel was no angel, either. She told me months before her wedding, she slept with my brother-in-law. She had an affair with my half-sister's ex-husband, Terrence Walker. Rachel slept with him and became pregnant by him. She also had a one night stand with my brother, Kevin. She admitted that to me after my father's cook-out, although she said that he only gave her oral sex. Well, in my book sex is sex! So much for Ms. Goody Two Shoes, Rachel Simms!

The night she told me about her affair with Terrence, it took everything in me to hold my tongue. Her selfishness had gotten out of control. She had the nerve to chastise me about the things I did when all the time, that heifer had gotten pregnant by a married man. I wanted to laugh in her face that night. I played the part of best friend and even went to an abortion clinic with her a week later. However, in true Rachel fashion, she couldn't go through with it. She really must have had God on her side when she miscarried the baby. Lord knows that if she had the baby, her marriage to Corey would have surely been over. Corey was too good for Rachel anyway; at least, that is what I used to think.

The Corey that I was seeing now was different. This cold, heartless Corey was going to feel my wrath. I had let him get away with this way too long. The days of his not being there for Mercy and not accepting her were over. Either he was going to man up or a judge would make him. If I filed paperwork on him, Rachel would surely find out. I didn't want it to happen that way, but I was just so tired. I was tired of living a lie and drinking myself to numbness.

I veered my truck onto the highway at the exact moment when the sky went pitch black and the rain poured down. I was en route to Vivian's house to drop off Mercy. Mercy spent most of the weekdays at my sister's house. Vivian said that she could take better care of Mercy than I; therefore, I didn't complain about Mercy being with her all the time. This was an insult to me, but she was right.

After the phone call with Corey, I downed three shots of Ciroc and loaded Mercy into the truck. Vivian lived twenty five miles from me without traffic. I was supposed to get Mercy to her house hours ago, but between talking to Corey and drinking, I had lost track of time. Once Mercy started getting impatient, I knew it was time to get rid of her. She was so restless that in order to deal with her and calm myself, I had to take my medication.

My wheels began to slide a bit on the streets covered with the falling precipitation. I was in desperate need of new tires but hadn't taken the time to purchase any.

"Maaaa, you going too fassst," Mercy whined from the back seat. "Slooow down!"

I glanced in my rearview mirror at my daughter as she poked out her lips. I forgot her car seat the other day when I picked her up from Vivian's, so I had to strap her down in the seatbelt. Vivian called me nonstop for two days to come back and get it. I didn't have time to be bothered with one little car seat, especially when Mercy could use the same seatbelt as I.

I focused on the road, ignored Mercy, and whipped my truck in and out of lanes. My beaten up windshield wipers made things worse by splashing the rain back and forth. I was still so pissed from the conversation with Corey that I didn't pay any attention to how fast I was going. All he was worried about was Rachel finding out. He didn't give a damn about his daughter or me. I wasn't the only one that was at fault the night Mercy was conceived, but I was the one that had to suffer.

I thought about calling Corey back. If he said one more thing to me, I was going to pack up Mercy and drop her off on his doorstep. Anyone with clear vision could see that Mercy bore an uncanny resemblance to Corey. However, I was able to convince Rachel that Mercy's father looked much like Corey. Rachel was not only selfish, but she was gullible at times as well. The first time Corey and Rachel came to my house a few weeks after Mercy was born, I was terrified that she would see the similarity between Mercy and Corey. I had just had Mercy and was trying to handle things on my own. Once Rachel and Corey arrived at my apartment, I couldn't even look at my best friend. I presumed Corey sat in his truck so he wouldn't have to look at Mercy. It was the first time of many that he didn't acknowledge our daughter.

"No more," I shouted, almost turning my truck on two wheels to pass a slow green Mazda going twenty miles below the speed limit. I blew the horn and gave the driver of the car my middle finger.

The more I thought about Corey's behavior, the more the heat from my anger made my truck feel like a sauna. I pressed the air control button so hard, part of my acrylic nail popped off.

"Shit!" I screamed, taking my eyes off the road and concentrating on my broken nail. I put my eyes back on the road and sighed loudly. It seemed like it was taking forever to get to Vivian's house. I pressed the gas and zoomed past another car that had gotten in my way.

Corey must have thought he was playing with a little girl the way he tried to handle me, I thought. Well, Mr. Corey Perkins, let's see what you will do once all your secrets and lies are revealed.

The liquor that I drank earlier was giving me an awful headache. I hadn't eaten anything, either. After talking to Corey, I really didn't have an appetite. I just needed my medicine to numb the pain.

As I put my signal light on to switch lanes again, Mercy began to cough in her sleep. I looked in the mirror to see if she was okay but my vision was blurred.

"Damn," I shouted as Mercy continued to cough.

My foot still on the gas pedal, I quickly turned to the back seat to shake Mercy awake. She was choking but not waking from her deep sleep. I glanced toward the road and then turned around again to shake her once more. She woke up still coughing and trying to catch her breath. I turned around to face the road in time to avoid hitting the back of a black Nissan Pathfinder. I swerved with so much force that my Yukon bounced from the middle lane to the left. Horns were blasting at me as I tried to steady my truck in one lane.

Slightly pressing on the brake, I slowed down and moved back into the middle lane. I took a deep breath and tried to regain my composure. I focused my eyes on the road and continued to move with traffic. I glanced at the eighteen wheeler that was to the right of me, and then the grey Cadillac that was to the left of me. My vision was still a bit blurry but I could tell that the eighteen wheeler was moving into my lane as if the truck driver didn't see me. I laid on my horn to get the truck driver's attention, but it was too late. The truck pushed me into the Cadillac and before everything went totally black, I remembered hearing a loud crash and Mercy's scream.

25

Corey

CHARLOTTE, NC

I paced around the kitchen listening to Rachel talk on the phone. This couldn't be real. This wasn't happening. Trying to hide from Rachel the fact that my hands were trembling, I sat down on the couch. I began to tap my foot nervously as I listened to the "uh huhs" and sobs from my wife. I didn't know whether to hold her or continue to sit like a lost puppy without any idea about my next move.

"Okay, we are on our way, Ms. Mary. Thanks and love you, too," Rachel said before hanging up her cell phone.

"Corey, we have to go." Rachel turned to me with tears in her eyes. Fear was evident all over her face and even though I tried to hide it, I was frightened, too. I had heard enough of the conversation to know that Rachel had been speaking with Ms. Mary, Von's mom, and that Von had been in a terrible accident.

She ran frantically to the room and began to throw random clothes into a duffel bag that was next to the bed.

"Ms. Mary said they are at Emory University Hospital about to have surgery," Rachel called from the bedroom.

"They? Who is they, Rachel?" I questioned.

Rachel reappeared in the living room. She walked over to the couch and sat down beside me. As tears streamed down her face, she grabbed both of my hands.

"Mercy was in the car with her. It don't look good, babe." Rachel let out a loud shriek, released my hands, and put them up to her face. She sobbed uncontrollably as I reached for her and pulled her into me. I couldn't believe what I was hearing. Mercy was in the accident, too? My daughter was hurt? For four years, I never acknowledged my own flesh and blood, and now she was in the hospital fighting for her life. Rachel raised her head and stared down at the floor. She wiped her tears, and in a matter of minutes, went back to the bedroom.

"If we leave now, we can be there right before they get out of surgery, Corey."

I wanted to respond and tell her that's fine, but I couldn't. I couldn't move or talk. It felt like all the wind had been sucked out of me and I was a mute. How could I have been so selfish all these years? The thought of something happening to Mercy had me paralyzed.

"Come on, Corey. Get up so we can go," Rachel pleaded from the room. I tried to tell my legs to move but they wouldn't. One tear fell from my eye and I wiped it quickly before Rachel came back out the room.

Seconds later, Rachel was standing above me again, telling me to get up so we could leave. She was mad, telling me how she was going to leave without me and that she couldn't believe I was going to make her go alone. She walked over to the bar where my truck keys were and grabbed them. My rattling keys must have sent a signal to my legs, because I was able to jump up. I snatched the keys from Rachel's hands and ran out the door in front of her. There was no way I was going to let Rachel go to the hospital by herself. Plus, I needed to make sure that Von and Mercy were okay.

I said a silent prayer and asked God to wrap his arms around my child. My child. Those two words kept repeating in my head as I pulled out of the driveway and began the four hour journey to Atlanta.

26

Rachel

CHARLOTTE, NC

*M*y heart was shattered. I couldn't recall the last time I felt this much pain. With the exception of my miscarriage, I had never been so heartbroken before; never been filled with so much sorrow and grief. Once I got off the phone with Ms. Mary, I wanted to crawl into a corner and just cry. I thought I would need Corey to pull over again so that I could throw up. My stomach was in one big knot and my head was pounding. I was so weak, and I couldn't stop the tears from flowing.

Over the years, I hadn't been the best friend to Von that I once was. I allowed my problems and what I was going through to keep me from being there for my friend. I saw the downward spiral she was in, but I never did anything extra to help her. She had always been there for me from my ups and downs with Corey to my affair with Terrence. She never judged me and still loved me. I failed as a friend to her. We would be on the phone and she would space out or sound erratic, which led me to believe she was on heavier drugs other than marijuana. I would use that as an excuse to call her less, but it should have been the other way around. That should have made me step up and help my friend.

Ms. Mary informed me that Von and Mercy were in a terrible accident with an eighteen wheeler. Von's family was at the hospital waiting for them to have surgery.

Von had suffered broken bones and a punctured lung. Mercy wasn't in her car seat but in a seat belt. Her condition was worse than Von's. I sobbed quietly as I thought about my goddaughter being hooked up to tubes and fighting for her life.

I cupped my cell phone with both hands. I didn't want to take a chance of missing a call from Von's mother. She promised to keep me updated on Von and Mercy's condition. It would take us four hours to get to Atlanta, which would seem like an eternity. Von would be out of surgery by the time we reached the hospital.

"Corey, can you drive faster?" I stared straight ahead and then down at my phone.

I was still very upset that Corey acted as if he wasn't going to Atlanta with me. Von had never been one of Corey's favorite people because of her wild behavior, but he tolerated her since she was my best friend. He had actually formed his own friendship with her. He told me that whenever my birthday or any other special occasion came around, he asked Von for help choosing gifts for me. I stared at Corey in disbelief as he sat on the couch, looking at his feet and not moving when I asked him repeatedly to come on so that we could get on the road. Time was of the essence and I needed to get to my best friend.

Corey stared straight ahead at the road and ignored my request for him to speed up. We had been on the road for an hour and sat in silence the entire time. I sat there sobbing silently and Corey hadn't said a word.

My phone beeped. A text message was coming through.

Hey beautiful flashed on my screen.

I had talked to Terrence earlier and told him I would hit him back later. I knew this was his method of checking on me.

I typed a quick response to inform him of what was going on and what hospital Von was in. I let him know that I would give him an update later.

Ok. sweetie, let me know if you need me flashed on my screen before I turned my phone over in my hands.

"I need to call Daryl and Monica," I said aloud to no one in particular.

I dialed Daryl's number first since he was already in Atlanta. Months ago, he suggested I check on Von more. He hung out with Von from time to time and noticed the changes in her. I regretted not paying more attention to my friend now.

The phone rang four times before Daryl picked up.

"Hey, D, you sleep?" I asked after he said a shaky hello.

"Nah, baby girl. Just relaxing a bit. What's up?"

"Brother, you sitting down?" I tried my best to hide the emotion in my voice.

"What's wrong, Rachel," Daryl insisted.

"Von and Mercy were in an accident. They are at Emory Hospital, Daryl."

There was a long pause before Daryl spoke again. "Are they okay?"

"They are getting ready for surgery. Just pray, D. We are on the way there, now."

"Okay, baby girl. Y'all be safe and I will see you at the hospital."

After I got off the phone with Daryl, I called my parents and Monica to let them know what was going on. By the time I got off the phone, I was exhausted from repeating the story and trying to answer questions that I didn't have the answers to. Never in a million years would I have thought that I would be calling everyone letting them know that my best friend and goddaughter were in critical condition and I didn't know if they would survive.

I laid my head on the headrest and closed my eyes. I repeated my prayer for Von and Mercy's full recovery.

It seemed like I had just drifted off to sleep when I felt the car stop. I opened my eyes and glanced out the window. We were parked in front of the hospital. Corey pulled up to the curb to let me out. I sent Ms. Mary a text to let her know that we were outside. Before I got out the car, I reached across the seat and touched Corey's hand. I needed consoling. I needed my husband. Corey stared straight ahead as if he was in a trance.

I sat there for a few minutes sobbing and then let go of his hand. I opened the door and put one leg outside of the truck. I glanced back at Corey. His head was now resting on the steering wheel.

"Baby, just pray," I urged. "We love them both. Just pray, baby."

Corey's body was shaking as he mumbled under his breath, "Lord, please don't take my child away from me."

27

Daryl

ATLANTA, GA

"Aye, man you gotta go." I pushed Jerome's head to get his attention. He looked up, his mouth full of my nine inches, and stopped in mid stride. He released me, saliva dripping from the corners of his mouth.

"Everything okay?" Jerome asked, his eyes full of desire. I could tell he wanted to continue our session, but he must have sensed from the phone conversation that something was wrong.

"Nah, man. I have to go—family emergency."

I pushed Jerome again from my lap and reached down to pull my jeans up. My mind was all over the place since Rachel called and told me that Von and Mercy were in an accident. Von called me the night before, and like I usually did, I had ignored her call. She only wanted to party and I wasn't in the mood last night. All I could think of now was what if I had answered the phone? Could that have made a difference today? If I was there, would she had been in the accident?

Those questions swirled around in my head. Jerome was talking, but I didn't hear anything he said. The only thing I wanted him to do was leave.

I had already gone against my better judgment by inviting him over. I couldn't concentrate because of the news about Von and I needed Jerome to get his things and get out.

While Jerome was taking his time to leave, I called Briana.

"Hey, hun!" Briana answered the phone cheerfully like always. Since it was early morning, my fianceé was at home most likely glancing over her lesson plan once more before getting dressed for school.

"Bri, I need you baby. Call in today and put on some clothes. I'm coming to get you. I'll tell you what happened when I get to you."

I hung up before Briana could ask me any questions. I glanced over my shoulder at Jerome who was now behind me, staring at me as if he was waiting on an explanation.

"You know, I am here too if you need me," Jerome said sarcastically.

I turned around to face him and stared at him in disbelief. I know good and damn well he wasn't jealous because I called Briana. "Are you serious right now?" I asked Jerome, moving out of the way so that he would have a clear path to the door.

"I'm just saying, man, you can confide in me, too." He walked up to me and tried to place his arms around me.

I jerked away. "Now is not the time and I would appreciate it if you would leave." My voice was steady as I stared at Jerome. This was the first time he was showing signs of being needy and I didn't like it at all.

Jerome gazed at me and raised his hands in a defeated way. "Aight, man, just hit me later . . . please."

"Aight," I said to Jerome's back as he walked out the door.

I told myself time and time again I wasn't going to deal with Jerome anymore, but as much as I prayed away the demons, my desire for him was greater than I imagined. However, after the obvious jealousy that he showed toward Briana, I had to let him go. No one or nothing would ever come between Briana and me. No matter what, I was going to make sure that she was going to be my wife.

I took a quick shower, changed my clothes, and hopped into my car to pick up Briana before I went to the hospital. Briana had met Von on several different occasions and always advised me to look after her more. She understood that we had a brother/sister relationship and was never bothered by it. Her confidence and secureness was another reason I loved her so much. I wished I had followed Briana's advice and watched Von more carefully, especially since she had Mercy, who I thought of as a niece. Mercy really looked like she could be a part of our family, too.

I pulled up at Briana's condo and blew the horn for her to come outside. Thinking of Von and Mercy made me get teary eyed. I said a little prayer that they would survive the accident. Von, if nothing else, was strong and a fighter. I had to believe that she would be okay. Once she was discharged from the hospital, I was going to make it my mission to call her more and make sure she was straight.

Briana came bouncing out of her house dressed in a pair of black pants and a pink blouse, and hopped into my car. Once she looked at me and saw the tears falling from my eyes, she reached for my hand.

"D, what happened?" she asked nervously. She placed her hand on my face and gently wiped away my tears.

I closed my eyes, breathed in, and then let it out. I removed her hand from my face, kissed it, and placed it on her lap.

"It's Von and Mercy. They have been in a terrible accident."

"Oh, no! Are they okay?"

"I don't know, baby, but we have to get to the hospital."

"D, do you need me to drive?" Briana asked, her eyes filling with tears.

"No, Bri. All I need is you to be right here with me." I backed out of her driveway and started our fifteen minute drive to the hospital.

"I am here, baby. I am always here," Briana said. She leaned over, her hair softly brushing against my face, and gently kissed my cheek.

28

Von

ATLANTA, GA

I slowly opened my eyes. The first person I saw was my mom sitting in the chair beside my bed, snoring softly. My mom's face was bare, without makeup, and her white blouse wrinkled, as if she had been sitting there for a while. A beige, dingy blanket was draped over her lap. I stared at her for a few seconds and then tried to move my head so that I could look around to see exactly where I was. The agonizing pain prevented me from doing that. My mouth was dry and it was extremely uncomfortable to even swallow. I struggled to stick out my tongue to wet my lips, but that was a failed attempt. The only thing that I seemed to be able to do was let out a groan. Surprisingly, making that sound made me feel just a bit better. I groaned a little louder, awakening my mom.

She jumped out of her chair and ran to the door, calling the nurse. "She's awake, she's awake," my mom screamed down the hall.

In a matter of seconds, I was surrounded by two nurses and a doctor.

"Hi, Ms. Singler. Are you feeling any pain?" the white haired surgeon inquired.

I could only respond with a slight moan. It began to hurt to even do that, so I stopped and just winked as a response.

Why was I even in the hospital, I wondered as I watched one of the nurses write notes in a folder and the other check the IV in my arm.

The doctor moved to the side. My mom was attached to him and looked over his shoulder.

"Should we be concerned about internal bleeding?" she asked in a hush tone. "It's good that she is finally awake, right?"

I attempted to listen to their whispers, but it was impossible for me to concentrate on what they were saying. The pain I felt in my throat moved to my chest, making it feel like someone had planted both of their feet on my breasts. The weight I felt was so intense that I began to cough and gasp for air.

The doctor ran to the bed and started speaking doctor language to the nurses. I recognized the words stat, blood pressure, and lungs before I fell into a deep sleep.

I woke up for the second time feeling a little better. The pressure on my chest had lifted and the relief made it easier to breathe. I had two tubes coming out of my nose, and my mouth was still incredibly dry. I smacked my lips and was able to stick out my tongue to moisturize my chapped lips. I glanced around the dark room and instead of my mom sitting in the chair, Kevin, my brother was there asleep. He wore his Singler Construction uniform and hat.

I started to groan, but I soon realized that I was actually able to open my mouth and make a sound. I attempted to call out my brother's name but the only thing that came out was the K sound.

I tried two more times with more force. On the third try, I was able to get his whole name out. Who would have thought that such a small thing like saying my brother's name would make me so happy?

"Kevin," I whispered.

Kevin stirred in the chair and opened his eyes. He squinted his eyes and once he seemed to realize I was awake, he rushed over to the bedside.

I smiled at my older brother and whispered his name once again. It felt so good to be able to talk.

"Hold on, sis, let me go get the doctors," Kevin said before running out of my room.

A few minutes later my mom, dad, Kevin, and Rachel followed a nurse and a doctor into the room. I was pleased to see all of them and shocked that Rachel had driven so far just to see me. I had figured out that I was in the hospital, but for what, I still had no clue. It couldn't have been that serious since I was feeling better and able to talk. The doctor again poked and prodded me, then pulled my parents to the side to inform them of something. I was sure that he was telling them that I was getting better and hopefully that I could go home. I searched the room and wondered where Mercy was.

Maybe Vivian had her like always, I thought. That's probably why she wasn't here, either.

Rachel and Kevin were standing next to the bed and I smiled at my best friend and brother. Both of their eyes were red and puffy.

"Kevin, can you call Viv and have her tell Mercy that mommy is okay. I know she is probably worried."

"Sis, don't try to talk so much," Kevin replied, grabbing my hand.

Rachel stood beside him wiping her eyes and looking down at the floor.

"Rach, I will be okay," I said. "You know can't nothing hold me down." I attempted to laugh but coughed instead, causing the weighty feeling to return to my chest.

Rachel moved to the opposite side of the bed and grabbed my other hand. "Just get some rest now, Von."

Before I could respond to Rachel, a loud cry erupted from the corner where my parents were huddled with the doctor.

"No, no, I won't believe it!" my mom screamed. She ran past my dad and out of the room. I tried to sit up to see what all the commotion was about, but the pressure from my chest was extreme and causing me to groan once again.

The doctor left my dad in the corner with his head down and walked over to the bed to stand beside Rachel.

"Ms. Singler," he began. He cleared his throat and continued. "My name is Dr. Kiser. You were in a very serious accident and suffered some traumatic injuries."

I shook my head and tried to understand what the doctor was saying.

"You might be feeling pressure on your chest, making it hard for you to breathe. That's because both of your lungs have been severely punctured. We have operated twice. You have suffered a lot of internal bleeding and your organs are just not functioning the way they should. Are you following me?"

The pressure had increased on my chest and I was unable to talk as much as before.

"Yes," I mouthed.

"We need you to get as much rest as possible and remain calm. Your condition is critical and we have exhausted all options. As medical doctors, we only do what we can and ultimately God has the final say." Dr. Kiser stood silent over my bed. I had a chance to digest his words. "Get some rest, Ms. Singler, and we will be back to check on you." He turned to look at my monitor and then slowly exited the room.

The doctor's words echoed through my head as I tried to make sense of them. Did he just tell me I was dying? I looked at Rachel and then at Kevin. Both of their faces were covered with tears. My dad was kneeling in the corner. The only person I could think of now was my daughter.

"Where is Mercy?" I asked, still barely able to talk.

Rachel and Kevin just stared at me, tears still falling from their eyes.

"Where is Mercy? Is she with Vivian? Why aren't they here?" I asked.

Kevin grabbed my hand. "Sis, she is still in surgery. She was in the truck with you. Viv is waiting on her to come out."

At that moment, it felt like someone had kicked me in my chest. "Is she okay? Please tell me she is okay," I pleaded with my brother. "How did this happen?"

Kevin shook his head and suddenly, his tears subsided. A frown lingered at the corners of his mouth. "You were drunk, Von. You did this," Kevin said, glaring at me.

"Kevin, please, I didn't mean to," I cried.

"My niece is fighting for her life because you didn't mean to!" Kevin said angrily.

"That's enough, Kevin." My dad rose from his kneeling position, walked towards Kevin, and placed his hand on his shoulder. "Von needs her rest." My dad guided Kevin out of the room, leaving Rachel and me alone. I continued to cry and wanted to explain, but the agonizing pain had returned, turning my words into moans.

"Calm down and rest, Von," Rachel instructed.

I couldn't argue with her even if I wanted to. I closed my eyes and fell into another deep sleep.

29

Rachel

ATLANTA, GA

Von looked so helpless lying in her hospital bed. I wanted to reach out, hold my friend, and tell her that everything was going to be all right. But that was something I couldn't do. The doctors had performed two surgeries on her and after the last one, they told us that all they could do was to advise us to pray. I was at the point where I was so grief stricken that I even started hearing things, too. When we finally made it to the hospital, I could have sworn I heard Corey say something about his child. I asked him to repeat it but Von's mom had appeared downstairs shortly after I sent the text informing her that we were there. She greeted me at the door and took me straight up to Von's room. Once I entered the room, I didn't leave. I wanted to be there for my best friend more than I had been the last few years and she needed me. Now, more than ever.

Von drifted in and out of sleep after the doctor revealed her fate to her. It broke my heart to hear her constantly ask about Mercy. As the godmother, I knew that it was my turn to step up and take care of her once Von was gone. I was preparing myself for that. This wasn't fair and my sadness had turned to anger. We are not supposed to question God, but why would he take my best friend?

After Kevin calmed down, he came back in the room to sit with Von. Von's mom and dad were in and out of the room, checking on both Von and Mercy. Mercy had successfully made it out of surgery and was in recovery.

I turned to Kevin, who was sitting in the chair beside Von's bed. "Kevin, you can get something to eat, if you want. I will stay here with Von."

"You sure?" Kevin asked.

"Yeah, go ahead. It will give me and my friend some time alone."

"Aight, I'm gonna head down to the cafeteria and then see if Mercy is out of recovery. You want something to eat, too?"

"Nah, that's okay. I'll tell Corey to get me something."

"Oh, yeah, that's right." Kevin grinned. "I have to keep my eyes and hands to myself now that hubby is here, right?"

I shook my head and gave Kevin a tired smile. "You crazy, just go," I teased.

Kevin laughed and walked out of the room. Kevin's remark reminded me of all the mistakes I had made before my marriage. Unfortunately, Kevin was one of them. We had a brief sexual encounter before I married Corey. Corey and I had had another argument about our wedding plans and Kevin came over to comfort me. I was so rude and nasty to him afterwards that I didn't think we would be able to restore our friendship. Thankfully, we did, and could laugh at what happened. The episode with Kevin was definitely something I regretted, however, the events with Terrence didn't fit into that category. More and more, I felt that I made an error not waiting for Terrence as he had asked.

Once Kevin left the room, I pulled my chair as close to Von's bed as I could and held her hand. She was sleeping and I didn't want to wake her, but I wanted her to know that I was there. I wasn't going to leave her like I had done in the past. I was going to be a better friend to her for as long as I could. For as long as she had left.

Von stirred a bit and slowly opened her eyes.

"Hey, sweetie," I said, letting go of her hand and gently moving the hair from her forehead.

"Rachel," she mumbled.

"Don't talk, Von. You need your rest."

Von turned her head to the side and coughed twice. "Rachel, where is Mercy?" she asked.

I wanted to cry every time she asked about her daughter. I couldn't imagine seeing her small body hooked up to so many machines. My plan was to check on Mercy as soon as the doctors would allow it so I could at least tell Von that she was okay.

"She is in recovery, Von. I am sure they will let you see her soon."

Von stared at me and coughed again. She grabbed my hand and held it tight. "Rachel, it's all my fault. Everything is my fault."

"Von, don't think about that," I said, tightening the grip on my best friend's hand. "Just relax and rest."

"I love you, Rachel," Von said with tears in her eyes.

"I love you, too, Von." I choked on my words.

"There's something I need to tell you," she whispered. It was getting harder for her to talk and I could see her blood pressure going up on the monitor.

"Von, don't try to talk. I think we need to get the nurses." I glanced at the monitor and noticed her pulse was speeding up as well.

"No," Von insisted, trying to sit up.

I stood from my chair in order to help my friend. "Von, if this is about Mercy, you know I will take care of her." I adjusted Von's pillows so that she was propped up a little more.

"Yes, it's about her. Please just listen, Rachel." Von shivered. I touched her hand and it was a lot colder than it had been a few minutes ago.

I walked around her bed to the closet to get another blanket to lay over her. I threw the beige hospital blanket over her chest and legs. Reclaiming my seat, I grabbed Von's hand again.

She looked at me and tears slowly began to fall from her eyes. "I never meant to hurt you," Von started.

"Von, you didn't hurt me. I was the one that wasn't there for you," I said, interrupting her.

"Rachel, please let me finish," Von whispered, barely able to get out her words. "I've done so many things I regret in my past, but I never meant to hurt you." Von was talking so low that I had to strain to hear her.

"You are my best friend and sister. I'm sorry. I'm so sorry." Von wept softly as the tears continued to fall.

"What are you sorry about?" I stood over Von and wiped the tears from her eyes. She was so cold and her blood pressure and pulse still hadn't gone down. I wanted to alert the nurses, but I didn't want her to get upset like she had done before when I had interrupted her.

"Rachel, I have lied to you and I'm sorry," Von cried. "I did something really stupid years ago and I've been living with it since."

I was more confused than ever. I had no idea what Von was talking about. I just wished she would hurry up and tell me so I could summon the doctor to check on her. I pulled the blanket up over her shoulders to warm her up. The room's temperature was close to 75 degrees. I was sweating but my dear friend was ice cold. She turned her head and coughed several times. I reached for the cup of water on her dinner tray and made her drink some.

She pushed the cup away after taking a sip. "That's enough. Please let me finish, Rachel," Von pleaded.

"Go ahead, Von," I said. I was getting more nervous about her rising numbers. I wasn't a doctor but I knew that her elevated blood pressure could not be good.

"I guess the best way to say this is to come out with it." Von paused to catch her breath. She placed her hands on her chest as if she was trying to move something from it.

"I think we need to call the doctor in." The way she was holding onto her chest was really scaring me.

"No, Rachel please." Von's eyes were filled with fear. "I need to tell you what happened. Mercy's dad is not some random dude I had a one night stand with."

I wasn't sure where Von was going with her story, but I wasn't going to interrupt anymore.

"Years ago, I made a huge mistake and I am so sorry," she said, beginning to cry again. She paused and then looked me directly in my eyes. My dear friend had lost so much weight that she looked nothing like the Von I used to know. She looked so feeble and small with her eyes almost sunken into her head.

"Rachel, Mercy is Corey's daughter," Von whispered.

I paused for a moment, not sure what I had heard. Von appeared to read the confused look on my face and repeated what she had just said. "Mercy is Corey's daughter."

"Huh? What?" I said, finally able to speak. I knew all this had taken a toll on me, but was I hearing things, too? I backed away from Von's bed. "What did you say?"

Von looked away. The tears were pouring from her eyes. "Before your wedding, Corey came by my house one night and was complaining about the problems that y'all were having. I don't know how it happened, but that was the night Mercy was conceived. Please forgive me."

I backed up towards the door, almost tripping over the chair that I had sat in, and looked at my best friend. I couldn't breathe. Was she telling me the truth? No, no, that's impossible. Corey and Von? I couldn't even imagine. Now was not the time to play such an evil and cruel joke.

"You are lying!" I spat at Von. "How can you not know how it happened?" I screamed. "You have to have sex with someone to get a child, Von. You know that all too well!"

"I know that," Von said between coughs. "It's true, Rachel. Just ask him. He has been giving me five hundred a month to support Mercy. I'm so sorry."

I didn't know what to think. My mind was racing. The missing money. So that's where it was going.

"Why would you do that to me?" I screamed, tears running down my face. "Why, Von? I loved you! You are supposed to be my sister! Why?"

Von tried to answer, but was coughing uncontrollably. I stared at my best friend clutching her chest, trying to breathe. The monitors rang out with warning bells and alarms. Before I could ask another question, three nurses and a doctor rushed into the room and over to Von's bed.

"Ma'am, we need you to leave," a red-headed nurse said, standing directly in front of me.

I heard her but I didn't move. I couldn't move.

"Ma'am? Please . . ." she repeated.

I forced my legs to take instructions. Head down, I slowly walked toward the door and out of Von's room. Von's mom and dad ran past me into the room while the doctors worked on her. I stood in the hallway, looking at the floor in disbelief. I couldn't collect my thoughts. Nothing made sense anymore. It was a lie, all a lie. I attempted to move away from Von's door, but one step had me on my knees, heaving and vomiting.

"Ma'am, ma'am, are you okay?" a nurse asked, running towards me. She reached down to grab my hand and helped me stand.

"Thelma, come help me with this lady," she called out to a coworker who was standing behind her desk.

I was so weak that I couldn't get up. I didn't want to get up. Von's words repeated in my head. Corey was Mercy's father. All these years, all these lies. With both nurses assisting me, they were able to lift me to my feet and carry me to the bathroom. Both ladies asked questions to find out what exactly my ailment was but I didn't answer. As soon as we entered the bathroom, I freed myself from their arms and ran into a stall. I closed the door behind me and hovered over the toilet.

"Ma'am, ma'am?" Thelma called out to me.

"Please, I will be okay," I mumbled from inside the stall. The nurses must have been satisfied when I finally spoke because they both left me in the bathroom. After I heard the door close, I collapsed on the floor. I screamed and cried at the top of my lungs until my voice abandoned me. For the next few minutes, I lay on the hospital bathroom floor feeling helpless, confused, and alone.

30

ATLANTA, GA

I was pissed! Not only did Daryl dismiss me like I was just a piece of trash, but he had the nerve to call his little bitch in front of me. He needed her all of sudden when I was down on my knees giving him top notch head. That's what I should have said to his simple, undercover ass. He was so scared of anyone finding out that he enjoyed sex with a man that he tried to convince himself that he didn't. All the talks of his demons were annoying. That was the last time he would openly disrespect me.

I hated to admit it, but I had really become attached to Daryl. I looked forward to talking to him and was slowly falling in love. I had never fallen in love with any of the men I'd had sex with in the past. I had deep feelings for Vincent, but I couldn't say that it was love. I was very young at the time and I didn't want to give up women just to be with him. I also had feelings for Freddie, but that was partially because of the years we had been dealing with each other and the amazing things he could do in the bed. However, I never wanted to be in an openly gay relationship with any man. But with Daryl Simms, I felt differently. I wanted to be more than just friends with Daryl. Daryl was the first man that I could see myself being in a relationship with.

His tall, lean frame which complemented his caramel-colored skin, had me falling in love with this charming man. That's why it hurt so much when he called Briana in front of me. It was a painful reminder that he would never be mine.

I was almost home when I received a text message from Freddie begging to come over. Ever since I discovered that he had called Pastor Simms, I had kept my distance from him. I questioned him about making the call, and when he wouldn't provide me a real answer, I told him that it was over. I didn't know what Freddie was planning by contacting the Pastor, but I would not be a party to it. My desire for revenge against Rachel slowly started to fade with my growing love for Daryl.

I knew I shouldn't have let Freddie come over, but I didn't get a chance to finish my session with Daryl and I was in need of some good sex. Hopefully, he wouldn't want to spend the night, but knowing Freddie, he would. I would just have to come up with an excuse to make him leave.

I took a shower and dozed off for a while before Freddie got there. Freddie came in and began to roll up a blunt before we got into our session. I was glad he had some weed on him. I needed to relax and clear my head of thoughts of Daryl, at least for a little while. I still wondered what the family emergency was that had him so upset. From eavesdropping on his conversation, I figured out someone was in the hospital, but I didn't know who. I wish he had confided in me. I could be there for him just as much as his little fianceé could.

Sitting beside Freddie on my couch, I flipped on the evening news and watched the reporters run through a couple of stories.

One camera flashed to a gruesome accident that had happened late last night on the Interstate. The wreck involved an eighteen-wheeler and an SUV that was so mangled, it was almost unrecognizable.

"Oh, no, that's an awful accident," Freddie said, looking up from his half rolled blunt.

"Yeah, it is," I replied. "I pray no one got hurt."

I continued to listen to the reporter talk about the deadly scene. My mouth dropped once the reporter revealed the driver's name.

"Did you hear that?" I asked, staring at the television in disbelief.

Freddie froze as well once he heard the name. "Did he just say Yvonne Singler and her daughter were in the accident?"

"So, that was Daryl's emergency," I mumbled to myself.

"Oh, so that's who you were with earlier?" Freddie turned to me and folded his arms across his chest.

I ignored him and listened to the reporter state that the victims of the deadly crash had been airlifted to Emory University Hospital and were in critical condition. Part of me wanted to go to the hospital to show Daryl that I was there for him. Show him that he didn't have to call Briana, all he needed was me. But the other part knew that showing up at the hospital while Daryl was with his family would be a very bad idea.

"Did you hear me?" Freddie asked.

"That's none of your business." I glanced at Freddie and then back at the television. I wasn't in the mood for Freddie's questions. If this was where the night was going, it would definitely end early.

"So, that's why I get kicked to the curb, huh? For perfect, little Daryl Simms? Wonder how the good Pastor Simms would feel if he knew that his only son is gay? Wonder if he would be so perfect then?" Freddie smirked.

I ignored Freddie, went into the bedroom, and picked up my phone from the nightstand. Even if I didn't go to the hospital, I had to let Daryl know that I was just a phone call away.

I dialed his number, and after the fourth ring, his voicemail picked up. I tried one more time, and finally, he picked up the phone.

"What, man? I told you I had a family emergency," Daryl barked.

I was taken aback by Daryl's rudeness. He had never talked to me like that before. Even if he was going through something, there was no need to be so mean.

"D, I just saw on the news what happened to Von. Man, I'm sorry. I'm here for you," I said.

"Yo, I have everyone I need. This ain't working out. I think it's best if you don't call me anymore," Daryl whispered.

"What do you mean, Daryl?" I was getting really nervous. The last thing I wanted was Daryl out of my life. "I know you are upset, but that don't mean we need to stop what we are doing. I have feelings for you."

"Feelings?" Daryl laughed. "Dude, you must be crazy! I mean it was cool and all, but I ain't got no feelings for you. I'm about to get married. We had fun but that's it." He continued to laugh.

"Don't laugh at me!" I insisted. "You mean to tell me all the times we were together meant nothing to you? Half the time you were in me raw and you felt nothing?"

"Man, chill, aight! I gotta go. Let's just leave this where it is," Daryl ordered. "Don't call anymore."

He hung up before I had a chance to reply. I stood there in shock with my phone in my hands. I couldn't believe that he was acting like that. I thought we had a real connection and he had the nerve to laugh at me. Laugh at me and my feelings for him. He mocked my love for him. I was furious! He was just like his bitch of a sister. They only thought about themselves and no one else. I had fallen in love with him and this was the way he treated me? No one would get the last laugh off Jerome! No one! I stomped around my room for a few seconds livid at Daryl. I sat down on my bed trying to calm down. Then, I remembered that Freddie was still in the living room.

I got myself together and joined Freddie. I sat beside him and gazed off into space. Freddie nudged me and offered the blunt.

"You okay?" he asked. "I wasn't trying to listen but I heard your conversation."

My heart hurt, but my pride hurt more. I took a pull off the blunt and let the weed relax me for a minute. I already knew what had to be done.

I turned to Freddie. "Let's just see what Pastor Simms will do once his son is outed on his wedding day."

Freddie's eyes widened. I took another pull on the blunt and closed my eyes. A plan was already forming in my head to get Daryl back for breaking my heart.

31

Corey

ATLANTA, GA

"Rachel, calm down! Stop!" I screamed while wrestling with her. I tried to pin her arms up against the wall to stop her from hitting me before security came. The older couple that sat next to me in the waiting room moved to the other side when Rachel rushed in and attacked me. I almost had her arms against the wall. In one quick motion, Rachel freed herself from my grip. She slid across the wall, circled around me, and was now behind me pounding her fists into my back.

"You lying bastard!" she screamed, punching me with all the power that she could muster in her body.

"What are you talking about?" I asked, turning around and trying to grab her again. I was confused and caught off guard by Rachel's attack. During our entire marriage, Rachel and I had never put our hands on one another. No matter how mad I was with her, I never dared to hit her. I faced my wife and saw a deranged look in her eyes that I had not seen before. Pieces of her hair that had been brushed back neatly in a ponytail had escaped and were standing on top of her head.

"Ma'am! Sir! You gotta take that out of here!" an older nurse shouted from the door of the waiting room. I knew it would only be a matter of time before security, or worse, the police, escorted us out.

I glanced at the nurse and raised my hand to let her know I had everything under control. The moment I took my eyes off Rachel, one of her wild punches connected with my mouth and busted my lip.

"Damn, Rach!" I cried out, touching the blood on my lip and using my other arm to block her continual punches.

Before I had a chance to restrain her again, a man ran up behind Rachel, grabbed her by the waist, and lifted her off the floor. Her arms and legs were dangling as she kicked and screamed to get free.

"Let me go!" she screamed, trying to break free of the strange man's grip.

At first, I thought the bald headed stranger, who was dressed in jeans and a button down plaid shirt, was a part of the hospital's security, but the fact that he was in plain clothes instead of a uniform let me know he was not a part of the staff.

I ran toward the unfamiliar guy who still had his arms wrapped around Rachel and had her up in the air. "Hey, man, let my wife go!" I demanded, reaching for Rachel.

"Your wife? Your wife?" Rachel screamed, kicking at me. "Don't you ever call me your wife again! You . . . you . . . lying, cheating, hoe!"

"Rachel, calm down," the man restraining her said. After a few seconds, she stopped fighting, so he put her down but continued to hold her around her waist.

"They are going to put you out of here if you don't settle down," he added sternly. "You need to be here for Von."

He finally let go off my wife's waist. Rachel tried to steady herself but was unable to and was about to fall down. In one swift movement, the stranger caught Rachel and helped her to stand.

"Aye, man, I got this now. Appreciate the help, whoever you are, but this is my wife and I can take it from here." I attempted to take Rachel from the man's grasp.

Rachel glared at me. "I wish you would touch me," she growled. "You might want to see how your daughter is doing. She is your responsibility now."

At that moment, my worst fears had come true. Rachel knew what happened between Von and me. Rachel knew that Mercy was my child.

"I . . . I . . . can explain," I pleaded, taking a few steps back. "Just let me explain."

"Explain what, Corey? Explain how you slept with my best friend? Explain how you had a baby with her? Explain how you have been lying to me for four years now? Explain what exactly, Corey? Explain what?" Rachel screamed, walking towards me.

The stranger followed Rachel and watched her movements. He seemed ready to grab her at any moment. I looked at him and again told him that we could handle this now. It was odd that he wouldn't leave and allow me to talk to my wife alone.

Rachel began to cry hysterically. She turned to face the man who had been following her and placed her head on his shoulder. He wrapped his arms around my wife as her body shook fiercely with every cry.

"Rachel, let's go," he whispered.

I didn't quite hear everything he said but I heard him call my wife's name clearly.

"Rachel, do you know this guy?" I asked as I walked toward them. I didn't appreciate how this stranger was holding my wife. I examined the bald man that was comforting her.

Her cries stopped and she turned around glaring at me as if she would have been happy to kill me right there in the hospital.

"You have no right to question me about anything." A slight smirk spread across her red face. "But if you must know, this is the man I should have married instead of marrying your sorry ass."

"What the hell you mean you should have married him?" I was in Rachel's face, looking down on her. She stood her ground with that smirk plastered on her face.

"Whoa, man, I can't let you do that," the stranger said, placing himself between Rachel and me.

I stood directly in front of the guy and was a minute from punching him in his face. I was inches taller than he was, so beating the black off him wouldn't be a problem. We glared at each other, silently daring the other to make the first move.

"Terrence, don't," Rachel said, tugging on the back of the guy's shirt. She yanked on his arm and turned him around so that he was facing her.

Two security guards, an older, black gentlemen and a young, slim, white man, entered the waiting room. They advanced toward us where we were making a commotion and seemed prepared to diffuse the situation. The older security guard waddled toward me and Terrence with his hand on his side, pulling at a belt that was hidden by his protruding stomach. The younger, skinny guard followed him closely, almost clumsily tripping over his own feet.

The older guard looked from Terrence to me. "Is there a problem, gentlemen?"

Terrence was still standing inches in front of me with his back towards me. He was facing Rachel as she tried to calm him down.

He glanced at me from over his shoulder and then at the guard. "No, sir. I was just about to take my lady and leave," he announced, looking at Rachel.

"Your lady? Man, that's my wife!" I screamed, pushing him. The push caused him to stagger forward into Rachel. Once he caught his footing, he turned around, smiled, and walked towards me.

The younger guard ran in front of Terrence and stopped him from coming any closer to me. Holding his hands out, the security guard instructed me to calm down.

"If y'all are going to leave, then go ahead, sir," the older guard demanded, pointing at Terrence.

I regained my composure a little once the guard reached my side. The last thing I needed was to have them call the real police and end up in jail in Atlanta. Nevertheless, I wanted answers about who this guy was calling my wife his lady. I took a deep breath and calmed myself down.

"I just want to talk to him," I assured both security guards, raising my hands in the air. Rachel and Terrence were standing off to the side beside the older guard. I began to walk closer to where they were standing.

"Stay right there," the tubby, black guard instructed.

I ignored the guard and kept moving forward. "Terrence, right? So what the hell gives you the right to call MY wife your lady?" I wanted to wrap my hands around his neck but I needed to know what was going on first.

Terrence stood there for a minute eyeing me. He glanced at Rachel, who had taken a seat in one of the waiting room chairs. Her head was down with her face in her hands, weeping softly.

He shook his head. "Man, just let it go. Don't ask questions you really don't want to know the answers to. All I am trying to do is take care of Rachel."

Fists clenched, I continued to walk closer to Terrence. "I don't need you or anyone else taking care of my damn wife!" My voice was louder than I intended but this dude was really pissing me off.

"Obviously, you do," Terrence smugly replied. "I should have never let her go."

The younger guard quickly stepped in front of me, cutting off my path to Terrence. "Rachel, what the hell is this dude talking about? You better tell me what's going on now!" I yelled.

Rachel looked up at me with tears on her face and remained silent.

"Since your secrets are out in the open, I guess it's time to put everything on the table," Terrence continued. "I never should have let Rachel go, especially when she told me about losing MY baby years ago. But now I have her back and I will take care of her the way you couldn't. Come on, Rachel, let's go." Terrence gently grabbed Rachel by the arm, lifting her to her feet.

At that moment, I completely lost all sense. I couldn't remember everything that happened, but after I leaped for Terrence, the burly, elder guard slammed me to the ground and wrestled with me. I was going to kill Terrence and no one would stop me. It took both security guards to restrain me. I managed to get up on my knees in time to watch my wife and this stranger, this guy, this man named Terrence, walk out of the waiting room together. Seeing them leave together caused me to lose all power. I stopped fighting and succumbed as the guards pushed me to the floor. I lay there feeling like my life had ended, and watching my wife disappear with another man, I knew that it had.

32

Daryl

ATLANTA, GA

I had played around long enough. It was past time to end things between Jerome and me. My wedding was less than a month away and there was no need for me to continue seeing him. I had to stay committed to Briana. I could hear the pain in his voice when I said those harsh things to him, but it had to be done. He knew that I wasn't going to keep sleeping with him after I was married. I allowed this thing with him to go too far, anyway. As the months passed, I saw him more and more. One or two times a month became once a week. I prayed and called my mom after every encounter with Jerome. For a few days after talking to my mom, I was good until something reminded me of him or until I had that itch I needed scratched. Now, when so much was going on with Von, I didn't have it in me to be cordial to him. Von was like a sister to me and it was killing me to see her in so much pain. The doctors had given up on her and it was just a waiting game until she passed on.

Briana and I sat outside in front of the hospital, not really saying much, but just listened to the night time sounds of crickets and other insects. I was at a loss for words and Briana knew me so well that she didn't force me to talk to her. She just simply held and stroked my hand. She was all I needed, all I wanted.

I slid closer to her on the bench and placed my arms around my fiancée. A tear crept from the corner of my eye. Briana wrapped her arms around my waist and laid her head on my chest.

We were sitting there in silence when, all of a sudden, I saw my sister and some man walking out of the hospital.

"Rach!" I called out to her. She didn't turn around or stop. She continued to walk straight to the parking lot.

I jumped up from the bench and ran towards her. The guy beside her held onto her arm as if he was trying to help her maintain her balance. I called out to her again, wondering where the hell she was going, especially with a stranger.

"Rachel, where are you going?" I asked.

She finally stopped and turned around to face me. I had never seen my sister with such a tormented look in her eyes. Her eyes were bloodshot and her face was covered with tear stains.

"Did something happen to Von?" I asked. "Where is Corey?"

A menacing laugh escaped my sister as she walked closer to me. I had no idea what happened but she was scaring me with her actions. Rachel approached me and stood maybe two inches apart.

She breathed in slowly and laughed again. "Von is dead and Corey is Mercy's father."

Rachel left to join the guy who was now standing beside a white Mercedes, obviously waiting on her.

"What? Wait, Rachel, what is going on?"

"Go ask him, D! I am leaving!" Rachel yelled before getting in the car with the guy.

I started to go after my sister but the guy drove off so fast that there was no way I would have caught up with them. I ran back over to the bench where Briana was still sitting.

"Baby, what's going on?" Briana stood up and grabbed my hand.

"I don't know, but I'm about to find out."

We returned to a vacant waiting room. I told Briana to have a seat while I checked things out. I walked down the hall to Von's room, but it was blocked off. I found a nurse at the nurse's station and asked her if she knew what was going on.

The young girl looked down at her chart and then, at me. "Are you a family member of Ms. Singler's?"

I nodded that I was.

"I am sorry for your loss," she replied sympathetically.

I hesitated for a second, dreading the next question I had to ask. "Did she pass?"

"Yes, about thirty minutes ago," the nurse said, on the verge of tears herself.

"What happened to the people in the waiting room?" I asked, remembering all the empty chairs.

The nurse looked down the hall to see if anyone was around or listening.

"A guy was taken to jail on a disorderly charge. Seems like his wife jumped on him," she whispered.

"Do you know their names?" I asked.

"All I remember is the cops calling him Corey."

I shook my head. The nurse's information meant that what Rachel said was true. My head began to hurt. I thanked the nurse and walked back to the waiting room where I had left Briana. When I entered the room, she jumped up. The look on my face must have told her that Von had died. She grabbed my head and squeezed it without saying a word.

Before I could tell her the details I had been given by the nurse, my phone began vibrating in my pocket. Maybe it was Corey or Rachel calling to tell me where they were, I thought. I pulled the phone out as Briana released my hand. She excused herself to go to the restroom.

Glancing at my phone, I saw that it was only a text message instead of an actual call. I opened up the message and I became so weak that I felt my knees buckle under me. I grabbed the arm of a chair to keep me from falling.

"God, no," I whispered as I looked at the picture on my phone. In the picture, I was in the middle of an intense sex session with Jerome. He was on all fours and I was behind him with a look of pure pleasure on my face. Under the picture, the caption read, "Wonder what Daddy would say if he knew?"

33

Rachel

ATLANTA, GA

I couldn't sleep. It felt like I was living in a never ending nightmare. After I left the hospital, I received one call from Corey. He left a message that he had been arrested. He deserved to rot in jail. I was so hurt by what he had done. It was one thing to get another woman pregnant, but my best friend? I thought about all the times that I talked to Corey about Von and Mercy. Mercy was my goddaughter, and now I'd discovered that she was also my stepdaughter. I was so feeble that Terrence had to carry me into his house.

Even though I was in pain, I was also truly glad that Terrence had been there for me. I had no idea that he was even at the hospital. The last message I texted him was that we had made it and I would keep him updated on Von's condition.

After getting off the floor of the hospital's bathroom, I made it to the waiting room with every intention of confronting Corey with the news that Von had shared with me. But when I saw him sitting there, and I thought of all the lies he had told me for four years, I only wanted to kill him. The next thing I knew, Terrence was picking me up and carrying me away. Once I calmed down, I heard Terrence telling Corey about our baby. At that point, I didn't care anymore. I wanted to hurt Corey as much as I was hurting.

Hours later, I was lying in Terrence's bed wearing a pair of his basketball shorts and his white t-shirt. I was drained and I couldn't even undress myself. He laid me on the bed, took off my clothes and dressed me in his clothes. He kissed me lightly on the cheek, tucked me in, and told me to try to get some sleep. That would be impossible, but I lay there and cried until I had no more tears. For hours, I tossed, turned, and thought.

My best friend was dead but I couldn't even grieve for her because she had betrayed me. Not only had Corey lied to me, but Von was dishonest as well. I couldn't just blame Corey, but what good would it be to hate Von when she was gone now? My entire life had changed in a split second and I didn't know how to pick myself up. My marriage was completely over. Everything that I thought was true had been all lies. I felt as if someone was continually stabbing me in the heart. The pain was unbearable. I stirred in bed, trying to get comfortable, but every time I did, I thought about Mercy. I didn't know how she was doing. The last update from the doctor was that she was out of surgery and was breathing on her own. I received that status a few hours before Von had passed. I tossed and turned for about two hours. I glanced at my phone and it was almost three in the morning. The house was silent and I wondered if I was by myself.

"Terrence?" I asked softly.

The house remained quiet. I didn't want to be alone anymore with my thoughts, so I called out to Terrence again louder.

After a few seconds, Terrence appeared in the doorway of his room. He stood there for a moment and just looked at me. I returned the favor. He walked towards the bed and finally broke the silence. "You okay, baby?" he asked.

His baritone voice sent chills down my spine. I stared at this beautiful man who was wearing a pair of basketball shorts and had his bare chest exposed.

For a second, with Terrence standing over me, the pain eased a bit. I was a mess, but he still was there. Four years ago, I made the wrong choice. I made a mistake when I chose Corey over Terrence. Even though Terrence was married at the time, I should have waited. I should have trusted my feelings for this man. Now, after all these years, who would have thought that we would end up together?

Terrence took a seat next to me on the bed and placed both of his arms around me. He felt familiar and different at the same time. I knew this man and had loved him once, but now we had both grown and were not the same. Even more so, the attraction and bond were still there. His arms were the only ones that could console me right now. I placed my head on his shoulder and exhaled. I closed my eyes, and right before the tears started falling again, I heard my phone ring. Since I'd left the hospital, I hadn't been in touch with anyone. Both Daryl and Monica had called but I didn't answer. I knew from the Donald Lawrence ringtone that it was my mom calling. I was sure that Daryl had informed my parents and Monica about what happened at the hospital. I didn't know what I was going to say to anyone or how I would explain this. I felt foolish for being lied to for so long by my husband and best friend. The pain was excruciating, but I had to talk to someone sooner or later. As much as I wanted to stay hidden away at Terrence's house, that plan was not realistic.

I reached for the phone and took a deep breath. "Hello," I answered.

"Rachel, are you okay? Where are you? Daryl told me what happened and you need to come home. We will fix this," my mom stated. She didn't pause long enough for me to get a word in.

"Tell me where you are," my mom continued. "I can't believe that all this was going on and you didn't tell me. If it hadn't been for your brother, I would have never known."

I interrupted my mom's rant, which was giving me a headache. "Mom, I'm okay."

"Come home, then, Rachel. You need to be with your family right now."

"Mom, I am home. I'm fine and I promise, I will call you later. I love you, Mom." I hung up without giving her a chance to ask any more questions.

I laid my phone on the nightstand, and as soon as I turned toward Terrence, it began to ring again. My mom's picture appeared on the screen, but this time, her call would go unanswered.

Terrence took my hands into his and starred down at them for a few seconds. "*Are* you home?" he asked, looking at me.

Without hesitation, I leaned in and placed a gentle kiss on his lips. Once the kiss ended, I stared at Terrence. I stared at the man whose child I once carried. The man that I had been in love with all those years ago. My heart was broken in so many pieces, I wasn't sure if I told my mom I was home because I was hurt or because I really wanted to be there with Terrence. The one thing that was clear was Terrence was the only reason I didn't feel the need to walk out in traffic.

"Yes," I replied. "I am where I should have been from the start."

Terrence released my hands and leaned in to kiss me again. His kiss made me remember why I fell in love with him years ago. He stopped suddenly and pulled back. I slid closer to him to let him know I didn't want it to end.

"Rachel, I know you are hurting right now. I don't want this to be some sort of rebound. I never stopped loving you and if we do this, I want it to be real." Terrence moved so that there was space between us.

I was silent for a moment, trying to gather my thoughts. Terrence was right—I was in pain. I was hurting more than I ever had before and I didn't want this to be a knee jerk reaction to something Corey and Von had done.

I slid closer to him and placed my hand on his leg. "Terrence, you are right. I need to feel loved, though. I'm lost. You are the only one who makes me feel like I am not hopeless. I need you . . . I want you. Please make me feel loved."

At my request, Terrence stood up and went into the bathroom. I heard water running in the tub. After a few minutes, he walked back into the bedroom and over to the bed. He grabbed my hands and pulled me up and guided me into the bathroom. Without saying a word, he undressed me and pointed toward the bubble bath he had drawn for me and ordered me to get in. At first, I was a little reluctant to allow Terrence to see my body. I couldn't hide the weight I'd gained over the years. However, he didn't seem to take notice or even care. I slowly walked toward the huge garden tub in the center of his bathroom and stepped in. The water was steaming and I had to get used to the heated bubbles. I sat down gingerly as the bubbles surrounded my naked body. The water relaxed me as I slid further down. I closed my eyes and allowed the aromatherapy candles that surrounded the tub to free my mind. This was exactly what I needed. I hadn't even heard Terrence leave and come back in until he whispered my name. I opened my eyes and saw Terrence holding a wine glass. I took the glass from him and sipped the sweet, red wine. I placed the glass on the outside of the tub, slid back down in the bubbles, and closed my eyes again.

"Sit up," Terrence instructed.

Terrence kneeled down beside the tub with a loofah sponge in one hand and a bottle of Cherry Blossom body wash in the other.

"You know that's one of my favorite scents," I said as I smiled at Terrence.

"It was here waiting on you," he said as he washed my back. He took the loofah and covered my entire body with the wash. His hand disappeared in the water and between my legs. I tilted my head back. My body was relaxed and I was enjoying every second of this. Terrence rinsed me off, stood, and left the bathroom. I sipped some more wine and sat the glass back down. I breathed deeply and exhaled. Who knew that a simple bath could make me feel better?

Terrence reappeared with a towel and bathrobe. "Are you ready to get out?" he asked.

I carefully rose from the water. Terrence reached for my hand to help me out of the tub. He wrapped the soft towel around me, dried me off, and then wrapped me in the white, fluffy bathrobe. I didn't have to move or do anything on my own. Terrence took care of everything. He grabbed my half empty wine glass and directed me to the bedroom. I walked toward the bed and sat on the edge. On the nightstand now was a bottle of Cherry Blossom lotion and some massage oils.

"How did you plan all this? How did you know I would be here?" I questioned Terrence as soon as he walked back into the room.

Terrence smiled and came toward the bed. "The first day we reconnected, I went and bought this stuff. I'm not trying to sound cocky or arrogant, but eventually, I knew you would be back."

"Oh, no, that doesn't sound cocky at all." I said sarcastically, rolling my eyes.

"Rachel, I meant it when I said if I ever got you back, I was never letting go. Now lie down on your stomach, please."

I did as Terrence requested. He removed my robe and squeezed a small amount of massage oils in his hands. He rubbed his hands together to heat up the oils. He placed his hands on my back and started the gentle massage.

Without a doubt, it was the best massage I ever had in my life. I moaned as he continued. He placed pressure on the tense parts of my body and released all my stress. I was in pure bliss.

"Turn over," Terrence said.

Once again, I did as I was told and turned over.

"You are more beautiful than I remember," Terrence said, taking the lotion off the dresser and rubbing it over my shoulders, breast, and down my stomach. He softly caressed my nipples as I let out another slight moan.

Terrence smiled at me, wrapped his arms around my legs and slid me towards him. He lowered his head and kissed my stomach. His tongue circled my belly button. After a few seconds of light teasing, he inched further down and stopped when his head paused between my legs. He started off slow by opening the lips of my vagina and placing his whole tongue directly on my clit. He went from using his entire tongue to just using the tip to flick at it. I wanted to scream for dear life; those little motions that made my body tremble. I climaxed about three times before Terrence stopped and looked up at me.

"Have you had enough?" he asked.

"Make love to me, Terrence," I begged.

"That will come in due time," Terrence said. His head disappeared between my legs again. While he tasted me, he caressed my breasts. He licked me so much, I had an orgasm so great, I felt it throughout my entire body. I screamed and pushed Terrence's head away from me. I turned on my side away from him, trying to catch my breath. Terrence pulled the sheets and blankets over me and kissed me on my cheek.

"Get some rest, baby," he said. He walked to the bedroom door and turned off the lights.

Still on my side, I smiled, and closed my eyes. Before long, I was sound asleep.

34

CHARLOTTE, NC

*T*ime was slowly creeping by and I was getting restless. Freddie went inside the church an hour ago, after the last member had driven off the parking lot of New Zion Baptist Church. Freddie and I had sat in the church's parking before he went inside, watching the cars and making sure that the coast was clear so that we could carry out our plan. I glanced at the time on the dashboard and then back at my cell phone in my lap. He should have been out by now, I thought, wondering what could possibly be taking so long.

A few days earlier, Freddie had set up a meeting with Pastor Simms to ask if he could join New Zion again. It was part of our plan to find out any information we could use to let the whole church know that Daryl Simms was bisexual. Pastor Simms was the talkative type. During their meeting, Freddie told me, one mention of Daryl's upcoming vows sent the Pastor into another thirty minute conversation about how lovely it was going to be. Freddie discovered that, during the ceremony, a projector would be set up to display Daryl and Briana's engagement pictures. I took that one piece of information and put our plan in motion.

Due to my lengthy stay at the hotel, I was privy to a lot of special options that most customers were not.

I asked the hotel to keep a camera in my room and was able to film all the encounters that Daryl and I had. I took the tapes, had converted to pictures, and put all the evidence on a CD. Freddie's job was to go in after the church meeting, switch our CD with any CD that might already be in the computer. He was going to label our CD the same as the wedding CD, so if anyone looked at it before the service, they would be none the wiser. It was a perfect plan.

I glanced at my watch again and more time had passed since Freddie went inside the church. I debated whether to go in and check on him or sit in the car a little longer. It shouldn't have taken that long to change a CD. I was parked in the front, off to the side, so I could see all the cars but they couldn't see me. Everyone had left an hour earlier and the parking lot was a desert. I started my car and decided to go around to the back of the church. Maybe Freddie had come out that way and was making sure that everything was set for tomorrow.

As I traveled toward the back of the church, I noticed Pastor Simms' car was still parked in his spot. That was strange, I thought. I could have sworn he left a while ago. Something was wrong. I continued to the parking lot behind the playground and where another car was parked. No one ever parked that far behind the church except when there was a revival. During revival, the parking lot was so full that the only other place to park was behind the playground. Something definitely wasn't right and the last thing I wanted was to get caught. I circled the parking lot one more time and decided to call Freddie to see what was going on.

After his phone went to the voicemail the second time, I decided that I would just leave. Something wasn't right and if Freddie had been caught by Pastor Simms, I didn't want my name in it. After circling the parking lot for a third time, I crossed over to the highway and started on my way home. I hoped that Freddie had enough time to change the CD and that no one saw him doing so.

35

Daryl

CHARLOTTE, NC

"Ma, don't worry. I'll go over and make sure things are set up," I said into my Bluetooth headset as I walked out of the club where my bachelor party had been held. My mom had been working nonstop on the wedding for the last few days and I wanted her to go home and get some rest. I was a little tipsy from my party, but not as drunk as the rest of my friends who celebrated with me. I needed to be at my best for the wedding; therefore, a drunken night was not in my plans, no matter how much my friends urged me to take more shots of liquor. However, what I had planned to do was go by the church for a last once over. A church meeting was being held there, so we had to reschedule our wedding rehearsal for Thursday instead of tonight. I wanted to make sure that all the flowers and decorations were set. Everything needed to be perfect for tomorrow.

"You know, I would feel better if I did that, son. You are the one that needs rest and I know you have been drinking. I will be fine," my mom insisted.

"Mom, no, please go home," I pleaded. "Where are you now anyway?"

"Okay, son, just calm down. I am leaving the reception hall now. We have done so much to get to this day. I'm proud of you, Daryl. Just remember that everything has been done to get you to this point. I am happy for you and Briana. You couldn't have picked a better bride."

My mom's approval meant the world to me and I was so glad that she was happy with the decisions I was making in my life. She had been there for me every step of the way and I was beyond grateful.

"Mom, I love you. Now, go home and get some rest so you can look beautiful tomorrow."

"Yes, son. Don't be at the church too long, okay?"

"Yes, ma'am." I hung up the phone and dialed my soon-to-be wife's number.

"Hey, baby!" Briana screamed in the phone.

"I see you're still partying," I said and laughed.

"My sisters and cousins are, but I am about to turn in for tonight. I have a big day tomorrow, you know," Briana said, her words slurred.

Briana didn't drink much, so if she had a glass or two of wine, she would always pass out.

"Yes, you do. Are you ready to become Mrs. Simms?" I teased.

"More than anything in this world. I love you, baby!"

"I love you, too. See you tomorrow."

I hung up the phone and thought about how wonderful my life was going to be with Briana as my wife. Thankfully, I hadn't heard anything more from Jerome since the night he sent the picture. I called him as soon as I had dropped Briana off and tried to reason with him. The fact that I was a lot nicer to him than I was before seemed to help. I even apologized and told him that I did have feelings for him, but because I was getting married soon, I just thought it was best if we became strictly friends.

Once he heard that I did care for him, he assured me that the pictures would be deleted. I was beyond relieved that no one would find out about him and me, especially my father.

I glanced at my watch and realized it was later than I thought. I was more than a little sleepy. I would stop by the church for a few seconds and then go home so that I could be ready for tomorrow.

On the way to the church, I got a call from my cousin, Terry, who was one of the groomsmen for my wedding the next day. He had another one of his emergencies and needed me to pick him up. His crisis always included some woman that he was messing with. Either her boyfriend or husband found out. Any other time, I would have told Terry that he had to take care of this himself, but I needed him in the wedding. I didn't want to take the chance that he might miss my big day. Thank goodness, he was only fifteen minutes from where I was. I picked him up outside a gas station and dropped him off at home after hearing about his adventurous night. He had left my bachelor party early to meet one of his women and neither one realized that she was being followed by her boyfriend.

"Man, one day I hope you settle down with one woman," I said as I pulled into Terry's driveway.

"Nah, cuz, I'll leave that one woman stuff to you. I got these chicks too deep right now. See you in the AM folk," Terry said, laughing.

"Be ready at nine," I hollered out of the window before pulling out of his driveway.

After driving another ten minutes, I finally pulled up at my dad's church. I drove to the back parking lot where I used to park beside my dad every Sunday. I pulled into my old parking space and was surprised to see that my dad's car was still there. The church meeting should have been over for at least an hour. Dad didn't linger after his meetings. After listening to the members argue and fuss, he was one way to his car and shooting down the road on his way home.

Over the past few months, my dad and I hadn't been on the best terms. He must have been in the room and overheard one of the many conversations I'd had with mom as she talked me out of jumping off the ledge. He felt the need to interject himself into the conversation and demanded that I stop all the whining and be a man. Men don't cry or whine. We do what we have to do. Ever since that conversation, I only said hello to my dad when I called my mom. He didn't realize that men had feelings and emotions too, and even if I tried to explain this to him, it would be a losing battle. He would never understand the demons I faced constantly. He could never know how I felt deep down inside or that he played a part in it. My mom told me time and time again not to think about it, but I couldn't help it. At least three times a week, I had the nightmares. They wouldn't stop.

I turned my car off and suddenly, an uneasy feeling came over me. Something didn't seem right. I looked around the parking lot and noticed another car in the very back behind the kid's playground. That neighborhood was home to Bloods gang members and usually, I would never visit the church so late at night. That was one of the reasons I didn't want my mom to go over there tonight. I opened my glove compartment and grabbed my gun. Most of the time, I didn't carry it with me, but for the last few weeks, I had been getting random calls on my cell phone in which no one said anything.

I didn't think much of the first few calls, but after receiving two or three a day, I began to think that it was more than someone mistakenly dialing the wrong number.

I tucked the gun into the back of my shirt and got out my car. As I walked around toward the back door of the church, the uncomfortable feeling grew. I glanced at the car in the back of the parking lot and noticed that it looked just like my sister, Monica's car. I opened the back door and tried to focus my eyes through the darkness. Searching for the light switch on the wall, I almost tripped over something lying in the hallway. I looked down at my feet, darkness still impairing my vision, and saw what looked like someone lying face down.

"Oh, my God!" I stumbled backwards and caught myself before falling to the ground.

"Dad! Dad!" I hollered into the darkness. I still couldn't find the light switch. I inched a little closer to the body to get a better view. It wasn't my dad on the floor. The man's body was much smaller than my father's, but I couldn't recognize who it was. I had to find my father to figure out what was going on. Becoming frantic, I quickly stepped over the body and walked in the direction of my dad's office.

Dad, where are you?" I asked, my voice shaking. I began to fear that something terrible had happened to him.

I turned the door knob to his study but it was locked. That was strange, I thought. He only locked it right before he was leaving. I backed away from his office and walked around the corner to the sanctuary. There was a dim light coming from the middle aisle. As I walked in, I saw the back of my dad. He was standing very still, watching something on the wall.

"Dad! "I screamed to get his attention. He didn't move or turn around. "Dad, what is going on?" I asked. "Someone is lying in the hallway, did you see . . ."

I suddenly looked up at what was holding his attention. "Oh, my God!" I yelled again. "No, no, turn it off! Please, just turn it off!" Pictures of Jerome and me were flashing as a slideshow on the wall of the church. Photos of every sexual position we had engaged in appeared over and over again, pictures of me behind him, him on his knees, and us on top of each other. How the hell did these pictures get here?

My scream knocked my dad out of his trance and he slowly turned around to look at me with tears running down his face.

"You disgust me!" he shouted, walking towards me. "This is the devil." My dad pointed to the slideshow on the wall. "YOU are not my son! YOU are the devil!"

My dad and I were standing face to face. "You are a disgrace! I can't believe you would do this to your family! You are not my son!" my dad screamed. "You want me to turn this off, huh? So I won't know the type of person you are? I didn't raise you to be like this!"

Tears fell from my eyes as the man who I admired, who I wanted nothing more than to be proud of me, told me that I was worthless.

"Dad, you don't understand . . ." I avoided his stare and looked down at the floor.

"Understand what?" he shouted. "That you are this . . . that you are GAY!" He pointed to the wall again.

His words continued to stab me and make me hurt worse.

"You make me sick!" He stood in my face as if he was daring me to say something. I backed up a little to give us room but that only made him step closer to me. Hate was on his breath as he stood directly in front of me.

"Please, Dad, stop, please," I pleaded. I was a disappointment to him, to my entire family. His words were like hands around my neck, strangling me, cutting off my breath.

"One way or another, I will get those demons out of you," he said, pushing me against the wall. My body shook and I was powerless from the tears that had my entire face wet. "Dad, please," I begged. I needed the torture to end and there was only one way.

I gathered just enough strength to pull the gun from the back of my pants. I pushed the heavy steel towards my dad, urging him to take it. "If I am the devil, then end my misery and kill me!" I continued to offer him the gun with the barrel pointed at me. I hoped my dad could end my life the way I had tried to weeks before. I didn't want to live like this anymore.

"What are you doing with a gun, Daryl?" My dad's eyes widened as he pushed the gun away. "What the hell do you think I am going to do with that? You are so far gone that the devil has you talking crazy!"

At that moment, in a blink of an eye, something snapped inside of me. My tears suddenly stopped and I stared at the man in front of me. This man, my father. The one that was supposed to protect me, but didn't. I looked my dad squarely in the eye. He wanted me to be a man and I was a man. He met my stare, baiting me to say something. "Give me that gun before you hurt yourself," he demanded, reaching for the gun. "Be a DAMN man!"

I loved and loathed my father at the same time. If it had not been for him, I wouldn't have been this way at all. He was the reason for the demons. He was the reason I was this way. If he had been the father I needed, my innocence would have never been taken away. I thought about the picture I kept in my wallet. The picture in which I was untouched and unharmed. The last photo that I had which reminded me of when I was happy and free. It was his fault. He stole that from me. He was never there. Those words echoed in my head, drowning out my dad's taunting. I backed away from my dad's outstretched hand as hate chilled my blood. Before he could reach for the gun again, I lifted it, turned it around, and pointed it directly at my father.

"What, what are you doing, Daryl?" My dad inched back, confusion on his face, with his hands raised.

"Oh, I am the devil, huh, Dad? I am evil and disgusting," I sneered. "Let's see how I got this way." I stepped toward him, still pointing the gun at his chest.

"Calm down, son," my dad begged. "Don't do anything you will regret."

"I am your son again?" I laughed. "Just a few minutes ago, I was nothing, but now I am your son again? You preach forgiveness and love every Sunday, but you don't believe that. You don't follow that you . . . you . . . hypocrite."

"I . . . I don't know what you are talking about, Daryl. Give me the gun and let's talk." He inched further away from the gun.

I laughed again. Just a few seconds ago this man that I called my father was insulting and ridiculing me, but now I had the upper hand. For the first time in my life, I felt powerful against my father.

"Daryl, baby, please put the gun down. I took care of everything," a voice called out from behind me. I slowly turned in the direction of the voice and saw my mom standing in the door of the sanctuary with a bloodied knife in her hand. Her white and purple shirt was drenched in blood.

"Mom? Mom, what happened?" I asked. I glanced from my mom to my dad, still pointing the gun at my dad. My mom looked like she had been in a boxing match with her hair stuck to her head with sweat. Her makeup had run down her face, causing black lines to streak down her face, from her eyes to the bottom of her cheek.

"I took care of everything, son," she repeated as she walked towards me.

"Mom, stop. Please stay right there," I commanded. She held onto the knife, which dripped with fresh blood. A disoriented look controlled her usually calm and smiling face.

"Deborah, what have you done?" My dad turned toward mom. "Did . . . did you kill him? Did you kill Freddie?" He stared at my mom and the knife as he waited for her to answer.

"I handled it, Robert. No one will mess up my son's day." She spoke sternly and reached for the gun. "Daryl, put the gun down."

My mom was beside me and reached for the gun. My dad lowered his hands and rolled his eyes at me. "Momma's boy," he mumbled.

I moved away from my mom and walked toward my dad. I didn't stop until I was inches from him and the gun was pressing into his chest. Tears were falling from my eyes.

"You want to know why I'm like this. You really want to know dad?" I cried. "I tried to tell you what was going on and you didn't listen. You never listened to me. I cried to you and you wouldn't even hear what I had to say. I was just a little boy, Dad."

"What are you talking about, Daryl?" my dad asked nervously. He tried to inch back, but now he was up against the wall.

"Baby, it's okay. Just leave and we will take care of the rest. I felt something wasn't right, so I came to the church and found Freddie changing your CD. Robert, you were in the study, so I handled it. He knew too much. He knew too much and had to be stopped. Please, baby, there is no need to bring up the past. You will only hurt more," my mom urged, running up behind me.

"Mom, no!" I shouted. "He needs to know!"

I still had the gun pressing on my dad's chest. He tried to move around me but I blocked him off every time he did.

"Your beloved Deacon Jeter," I started. "I was only twelve. I was so innocent. He took that from me. He took my innocence!"

"Stop with the lies. Stop! No, you will not tell lies!" my dad screamed.

"Lies? I tried to tell you, Dad. I tried. Ask mom!"

"Robert, Daryl, please we can talk about this at home. Let's just go home." My mom tugged on my arm. I had all my strength back, making it impossible for my mom to move me to get the gun.

I pressed the pistol harder into my dad's chest. "I am trying to tell you that he hurt me and you called me a liar. Every Sunday, you stand in the pulpit and preach, but you are no better than anyone else. You knew and did nothing!"

"You were a liar then and you are a liar now," my dad barked at me. "Nothing happened! You just wanted me to stay home with you and I couldn't. I had a church to run. People depended on me!"

"*I* depended on you, Dad! After I tried to tell you and you wouldn't listen, I couldn't bring myself to tell anyone else, not even Mom. Mom knew something had happened but she didn't know who. Every Saturday, he came over and fixed things and he would take me out back and touch me. He stole every good thing in me!"

I looked past my dad. The photos on the wall turned into Deacon Jeter and me. Before he became a deacon, he was an alcoholic. He came to New Zion in need of help and went into a twelve-step program. Once he finished the program, my dad would give him odd jobs around the house to help him get on his feet. He had everyone fooled that he was sober, but I knew differently. He would be drunk every other Saturday and come to the house, take me in the back and take my manhood. Every time it happened, I tried to tell my dad and he did nothing.

He told me to show no emotion and be brave and stop making things up. Dad took Deacon Jeter under his wing and made him a deacon. I was too ashamed to tell my mom, but she saw the change in me. Deacon Jeter told me that he would beat me into unconsciousness if I told and I believed him. My mom tried to protect me, but she never knew it was Deacon Jeter who was causing me so much pain. The abuse lasted for two years; two years, I endured that man raping and beating me. His demons created mine.

Everything became a blur and the room began to spin. I felt Deacon Jeter's hand on the back of my neck, forcing me down, forcing his dirty penis in my mouth. I cried, I pleaded, but no one heard me. No one. I looked at my dad, the one who was supposed to protect me. He was still not there. I wanted the memories to go away. I wanted it to end. My heart and soul couldn't take the accumulation of hurt anymore. I was tormented, divided, and I couldn't live like this any longer. The last thing I heard before everything went black was the sound of my gun going off.

36

Rachel

CHARLOTTE, NC

New Zion Baptist Church on this brisk Saturday afternoon was packed to capacity. Any normal Sunday, the church that could hold a thousand members never filled up with people. Revival Sundays were the only time, other than today, that the sanctuary was crowded. Today, New Zion was standing room only. People were literally sitting on top of one another and other members lined the walls. Some were in the vestibule of the church while others had taken seats in the offices at the rear of the church. Those that could not fit in the sanctuary were standing outside just to be in the midst. People began to seat themselves inside the temple at noon, although the service did not start until two o'clock. The time was now one-thirty and everyone was waiting for the family to arrive.

"Hey, hey, man, you got the camera ready? I want the first shot of the family coming in, if possible," Chuck, the news anchor for Channel 9 local news advised Gregg, his camera man.

"Yeah, I'm ready," Gregg replied, readjusting the lens on his camera.

Chuck was beyond giddy at the fact that Channel 9 was the only news station that had been granted access to the service. The station's ratings would skyrocket, right along with his career, once he covered the service of the decade.

"I can already see the new Mercedes parked in my driveway," Chuck said smiling. He continued to ramble about the car he would be able to buy with the promotion he was certain to get after covering this story.

"The police still looking to question the Baxter guy too?" Gregg asked, interrupting Chuck's chatter about his desired vehicle.

"Yep, there are reports he might be in Virginia," Chuck said. "Good thing Freddie kept a journal with all the details of him and Jerome's plans. Otherwise, dude would have gotten away scot-free."

Gregg shook his head. "The police will find him sooner or later."

"If we could crack that story first it would mean mo' money, mo' money, mo' money!" Chuck exclaimed. "A new Range Rover could go right along with my new Benz. I'd look good in a shiny red one."

The black hearse slowly driving up the church's parking lot stopped Chuck's talks of car colors. "Here they come, get ready!" Chuck instructed Gregg as he fixed his tie and took one last glance in the van's mirror.

I sat in the family car, not sure if I wanted to go in. After Von's death and finding out that Corey was Mercy's father, I took a leave of absence from work and stayed in Atlanta with Terrence. I spent many nights crying with Terrence beside me wiping my tears. He was my support system and treated me like a queen. I even had the chance to meet his three amazing kids: Stacy, Brandon, and David. All three kids were preteens and full of life, but Stacy was the youngest and her smile could ease the hardest hearts. I cried myself to sleep one night and Terrence had the idea of taking his kids and me to Six Flags. At first, I was hesitant, thinking they would remember me from years ago at Von's dad's cook-out. Once I saw Stacy's smile and realized that they did not remember me, I was on board. That day, I had the most fun I had experienced in years. As I was about to face one of the hardest days of my entire life, I thought back to the moments with Terrence.

Terrence and I came to Charlotte a week ago for my brother's wedding, and never in a million years would I have guessed that just a few short days later, we would be attending a funeral instead. Not just any funeral, but the home going service for the first man I ever loved. Without Terrence by my side for the last week, I would have lost my mind. The saying "when it rains, it pours" was an understatement. I had experienced too many tragedies in my life lately.

Everyone was out of the family car but me. I asked Terrence to drive his truck to the church instead of riding with me in case I broke down and needed to get away from everyone. He promised that he would be inside and close by for me. I adjusted the sunglasses on my face and put my hand on the door. I didn't have the strength to open it. I placed my hand back in my lap.

Monica knocked on the window and then opened the door across from me. She poked her head inside and looked at me. "Sis," her voice cracked. "Are you ready?"

I shook my head and looked back down at my hands. A tear rolled down my face. Monica closed the door and came around to the other side where I was sitting. Opening the door, she reached for my hand and gently pulled me out the car. I tugged at my black, wrap dress, and then caressed the heart of the silver necklace that Terrence had given me. I twisted it to hang in the middle of my chest.

Monica and I held hands as we walked up the stairs of the church to join Tony, Monica's husband, and my mom at the front of the line.

My mom's brother, Uncle George, stood next to her with his arms around her. Monica and I were behind them and Tony stood behind us. As devastating as this day was, my mom was poised and beautifully dressed in a black, two-piece suit decorated with beads on the shoulders and around the neck. On her head was one of the grandest black hats I had ever laid eyes on. Her hat was adorned with beads. Attached to the brim was a thin black veil that covered half of her face. She held her head high like my dad had always instructed her to do in the early years when he first went into the ministry. They are always watching, Mrs. Simms, he used to recite to her.

Pastor Robinson, a good friend of the family, was in front of my mom, leading the family in. "I am the resurrection and the life, saith the Lord. He that believeth in me, though he were dead, yet shall he live and whosoever liveth and believeth in me, shall never die." Pastor Robinson continued as we walked in. "I know that my redeemer liveth, and that he shall stand at the latter day upon the earth."

"I can't believe that this happened," I heard someone mumble to the right of me.

"Girl, you never know what goes on behind closed doors. It's just so sad. You know they are still looking for that other guy too," another person added.

I blocked out the whispers and looked straight ahead at the white and gold trimmed casket at the very front of the church. We were down the aisle now waiting as my mom viewed the body.

"Jesus, my Jesus!" my mom screamed. Uncle George caught her just before she passed out. He took her to the side and sat her on the front pew. Monica and I were up next to view the body.

"No, Lord," Monica cried. "Nooooooo!"

I gazed at my dad lying in the casket, stiff, eyes closed. My eyes filled with tears as I stared at him. My mom had selected his favorite black suit for him to wear today. He had a fresh haircut with more gray on the top rather than his usual black and gray mix. He looked so handsome lying there, as if he was just sleeping. I reached out and touched his face.

Tony held Monica and tried to move her away from the casket. I stood there for a moment. I couldn't move. My legs started to shake and I felt like I was going to faint. I leaned over the casket to place a kiss on my father's forehead. Turning around, I couldn't keep my balance. I let out a cry and before I knew it, like at the hospital, I was in Terrence's arms.

He had been sitting on the front pew on the opposite side of the family, waiting on me like he had promised. He carried me to the seat beside my sister and mom. I laid my head on his shoulder and cried.

The service went on and I heard parts of my dad's favorite songs. The hymn choir stomped and sang, "Guide me, oh thy, Great Jehovah", as the church members joined in rocking back and forth. One person after the next stood up and told everyone their fond memories of Pastor Simms. Each person was only supposed to talk for two minutes, but no one held to that. After the fifth person stood up and spoke for twenty minutes about how my dad had changed his life, it was finally time for the eulogy.

Pastor Robinson stood behind the podium as he waited for the cries to quiet down. "For those that didn't know Pastor Simms personally, you missed out on knowing an angel sent from heaven," he said. He cleared his throat and continued. "Today, church, while we are sad for having to say goodbye to our pastor, husband, father, uncle, cousin, and friend, we can REJOICE, knowing that Pastor Simms is definitely sitting on the right hand of God looking down on us! We might not understand why, but God knows what's best."

With my head still on Terrence's shoulder, I tuned out the rest of Pastor Robinson's message. It wasn't right that my father was dead. My dad was dead and my brother was in jail for killing him. My mom was there the night Daryl shot my dad. She tried to explain things to us, but they made no sense.

Two days before the funeral, I went to the jail to visit my brother.

I tried to talk to Daryl. He didn't say a word. He just stared off in space. He wouldn't even look at me. I asked God for understanding, but I never got it.

In a few short months, I had lost my best friend, my dad, and now, my brother. He confessed to killing both Freddie and my dad. His lawyer was fighting for an insanity plea so that he would get life in prison instead of the death penalty.

Any judge could see that my brother had to be out of his mind to kill his father and another church member. The only explanation that my mom gave us was that Daryl had snapped. What drove him to that and his motives she wouldn't say. I could tell that she knew more than she was saying, but getting my mom to tell on her precious baby would be impossible. Both Monica and I knew that Daryl had always been mom's favorite.

After the service, I vaguely remembered going to the graveyard and then back to the family car. The news crew was outside talking to several members, asking for statements. My mom had agreed to allow them to cover the funeral as long as they didn't ask to speak to anyone in the family. My dad had friends in many different locations and for those that couldn't come to the funeral, my mom wanted to grant them the opportunity to see the last goodbyes for my father. I had had enough of the television news, newspapers, social media, and Internet. The day after my father was killed, every lead story on television was "Prominent Pastor and Community Leader Pastor Simms: Killed by the hands of his only son." I wanted to turn everything off, including my mind and heart, so I couldn't think or feel anything anymore.

At the gravesite, I caught a glimpse of Corey standing beside his mom. He looked as if he wanted to say something to me, but with Terrence by my side, he kept his distance. His texts and calls were constant after he was released from jail. He must have realized that I was not going to answer, so he only called every once and a while. However, he did reach out to me when he heard about my dad. I talked to him briefly and thanked him for calling.

Mrs. Mary also called a few days before once the word got out about my dad getting shot.

I couldn't bring myself to go to Von's funeral. After everything came out about Corey being Mercy's dad, she told me she understood my dilemma about not attending. I couldn't fake it. I felt betrayed by Von and I couldn't force myself to go to the funeral. The only bright light in the entire situation was that Mercy had survived. She was such a fighter, and no matter how much I despised what Corey and Von had done, I couldn't hate Mercy. I loved that little girl from the first time I saw her, and just because her parents had done something awful didn't mean that she was a mistake. I thanked God that he had spared her little precious life.

Once we got back to my mom's house, I asked Terrence for a minute alone. I traveled up the stairs to my old bedroom and opened the door. My mom had barely changed anything in our rooms, so, my bedroom was almost exactly the way I left it with the exception of a few items that she stored, such as her old sewing machine. I smiled as I glanced at the poster of Tupac that was still on my wall. I had a major obsession with the late rapper while I was in high school. My mom fussed a lot when I put up the poster. Even though she hated it, my mom never took it down. On my bed sat five stuffed animals—two were gifts from my high school sweetheart. I sat beside the stuffed, pink monkey on my old bed, which was still decorated with a purple flower comforter, and reflected on the recent events. Everything happened so fast, from Von dying to my dad getting shot, that I hadn't had a minute to just think. I was familiar with the saying that God wouldn't put more on you than you could bear, but I was certain that this was too much for anyone to handle.

A few minutes passed and there was a gentle knock at the door. I looked at the door but didn't move to open it. After a couple of seconds, Terrence opened my bedroom door and came in.

"Rachel, I know you asked for some time alone," Terrence said, closing the door behind him. "I just wanted to check to make sure you were okay." He joined me on the bed.

I didn't answer Terrence or even look at him. I remained silent, my hands tucked underneath me and my head down. Terrence didn't say anything else; he just wrapped his arms around me like he had done so many times before. For the next few minutes, I sat in my room and cried. I cried for my marriage, my friend's and husband's betrayal, my dad, and my brother. My family was broken and would never be the same. A huge part of me was gone and would never be replaced. Divided, torn, and tortured, my soul would never be the same. Terrence lifted my head and dried my tears.

"Rachel, you have lost so much, but I am here. I love you and I promise I'm not going anywhere," he whispered.

I rested my head back on his shoulder, closed my eyes, and believed his words.

Epilogue

The sun's golden rays greeted me as soon as I parked my car and walked on the porch of the house that Corey and I once shared. Not much had changed on the outside of my former home. The grass, however, did look as if it had just been cut and the hedges were neatly trimmed. I didn't think Corey would be there since it was around nine in the morning. But when I pulled up, his truck was sitting in the yard sprinkled with the morning dew as if it hadn't moved all night or morning. I thought about calling him first and letting him know that I was coming to get the rest of my stuff, but decided against that.

Six months had passed since the funeral of my father, Pastor Robert Simms, and even though I missed him terribly, things were finally starting to slow down in my once turbulent life. The news coverage, rumors, and gossip about the deaths of my father and Freddie had died down and my family was finally getting some peace. Daryl had been moved to a mental institution after a failed suicide attempt in jail. My mom was the only one who could get a few words out of him when she visited. The anger at Daryl was slowly fading as well. I still didn't understand what led him to do such a horrendous act, but I continued to pray for my brother.

I was beginning to feel more like myself, so it was time for me to tie up all my loose ends, including those between Corey and me. I came to the house to serve him with the divorce papers and get the few items I had left before I moved to Atlanta to be with Terrence. Over the last few months, the love between Terrence and I had grown into something more powerful than I had ever experienced before.

I thought I couldn't love someone as much as I had loved Corey on our wedding day, but I was completely wrong. Terrence's love taught me how to enjoy the moments because tomorrow was not promised. His love made me a better woman, and I totally and utterly adored Terrence Walker.

I rang the doorbell and patiently waited for Corey to open the door. Even though I still had the key that he insisted I keep, I wasn't going to walk in without knocking first. I hadn't spoken or seen him in months since my dad's funeral. He sent a text every so often, but I believed he had given up the fight to get me back. He knew as well as I did that too much damage had been done to even try and reconcile our marriage. What was done was done and now it was time to finalize things for good. It had been my idea to move and leave Corey the house. Even though the house was in both of our names, I gave up all rights to the property. He could sell it or keep it. A sin is a sin, and as much as I hated what Corey and Von had done, I was no better with what Terrence and I had done, either. Self-evaluation is sometimes the hardest and I couldn't deny that the fact I had been in love with another man my entire marriage, and that contributed to the downfall.

As I stood waiting on the door step, I heard voices in the house, but no one came to answer the door. After a few seconds, I opened the screen door, which was always unlocked, and knocked on the door. I heard little footsteps running to the door. The door opened and standing there looking like an angel was my goddaughter, Mercy.

"Mercy, you know you're not supposed to open the door without me," Corey yelled from down the hall.

"Godmommy, Rachel!" Mercy screamed, and jumped in my arms. She threw her arms around my neck and hugged me so tight that I couldn't help but laugh. I hadn't seen her since she was in the hospital and my eyes filled with tears as I held onto her small body.

"Hey, sweetie," I said, hugging Mercy back.

I was surprised to see her at Corey's, but a part of me was glad he had stepped up and was now a part of her life. She had already lost her mother, and even though she was just learning Corey was her father, she didn't need to lose him, too.

Corey stood in the door for a moment with a stunned expression on his face. "I didn't expect to see you," he said, motioning for me to come in.

"I know. Hope I didn't catch you at a bad time." I walked in and placed Mercy on the floor.

"No, it's never a bad time. Mercy, let daddy and godmother talk for a second. Get our puzzle ready because we're gonna put it together in a minute."

Mercy hesitated and then looked up at Corey. "Daaaad, can I show godmommy some of my toys?" she whined.

"Yes, precious, in one minute. Now hurry and get in the room." Corey playfully chased Mercy down the hall. To hear her laughter made me remember all the good times Von and I had shared growing up. I walked over to the bar and glanced into the kitchen where I had once cooked endless dinners for Corey and me. I placed my purse on top of the bar and stepped into the living room to have a seat on the couch.

Corey came back into the living room and sat down on the couch beside me.

"I am glad that you are in her life now, Corey." I glanced around the house and noticed that not much had changed inside since I left, much like the outside.

"The only thing missing is you," Corey replied, sliding closer to me on the couch.

I stood and walked towards the bar near the kitchen. "That's what I wanted to talk about."

I reached in my purse and handed Corey the envelope that contained our divorce papers.

He put it on the couch. "I know what this is. Rachel, is there any chance for us? Any hope? We both were wrong . . ."

I stopped Corey before he had a chance to continue. "Yeah, I am no angel, Corey. Before we were married, I had an affair with Terrence, just like you had an affair with my best friend," I admitted. "I regret the things I did, but we can't change the past. All we can do is learn from our mistakes and move on." It was time that I was transparent with Corey. There were no more reasons to lie and keep secrets.

"One time does not make it an affair, Rachel."

"But one time makes it one time too many," I shot back.

"Was the baby you lost really his?" Corey's eyes begged me to say, "No, it wasn't," but I couldn't lie to him anymore.

"Yes, yes, it was his. It happened during the time before the wedding when we had gone for months without seeing each other." I lowered my voice a little. "It was his." I knew my words would hurt, but it couldn't compare to the pain I felt finding out Mercy was his.

Corey avoided my eyes and stared at the floor.

"Too much has happened," I said. "I wish you nothing but the best."

Corey looked up again and stared at me. "Will you keep in contact with Mercy?"

"Yes, she is innocent in all this and I won't make her pay for you and Von's mistake."

I walked toward the door and called for Mercy to come back into the living room. As if she was waiting for us to finish, she ran down the hall and jumped back into my arms.

"Godmommy, when you comin' back to play with me?"

"Soon, baby." I kissed her little cheek and put her down. Mercy looked up at me, and at that moment, in her eyes, I saw my best friend, Von. I would never know the reasons for her betrayal, but somehow, someway, I had to make peace with it. This little girl was a gift from God, no matter how she was conceived. She had almost lost her life in an accident, and for her to still be alive only meant that God had a plan for her. I bent down and gave Mercy another kiss on her forehead.

"I love you, Godmommy!" Mercy exclaimed.

"And Godmommy loves you too, pumpkin," I assured her.

I stood up and looked at Corey. Our eyes met. "Rachel, I still love you, too," Corey confessed.

I didn't say anything, at first, but just stared at the man that I had pledged to love for the rest of my life. The man that I took vows with before God and our family and friends. We had both made fatal mistakes, and for years, I tried to blame Corey for my actions. However, the only person that I could fault for anything that I did was myself. I thought I was being punished for my actions, but in reality, life happened. We take the good with the bad and keep moving. We learn to cherish every moment that we are blessed enough to have because in a wink of an eye, it can be gone. Tomorrow is never promised.

As all those thoughts went through my head, I smiled at Corey. I walked closer to him and grabbed his hand. "I will always love you." I stood on my tiptoes and placed a tender kiss on his cheek. Corey closed his eyes. He seemed to live in the moment.

Letting go of his hand, I turned and walked out the door. I jumped in my car and took one last look at the house that I had shared with my husband.

A tear gathered in the corner of my eye and slid down my cheek. That tear wasn't due to sadness, but due to closing a chapter and moving forward. That tear was one of joy. I buckled my seat beat and looked behind me to make sure no cars were coming.

Backing up my car, I thought about the happy times that Corey and I had. I put my car in drive and thought about all the wonderful days awaiting Terrence and me. For we remember the old to move on to the new, and I was ready for every bit of what was to come.